Persuading the Captain

AN AUSTEN INSPIRED ROMANTIC COMEDY
Austen Book 3

Rachel John

Copyright © 2020 Rachel John
All rights reserved.

ISBN: 9798647102980

ACKNOWLEDGMENTS

For all the Captain Wentworths out there, especially mine.

CHAPTER 1 ♥ HAVE YOU SEEN THE NEIGHBOR YET?

Anne patted her aging Mercedes on the dashboard, as if she could soothe the beast. The rattling was getting worse. Someone with more money and a better sense of timing would have taken it into an auto shop by now, but she just needed it to make this last trip to Big Bear Lake. She'd be there long enough to regroup and figure things out, including how to trade in her high-maintenance vehicle for something a little more practical.

She turned down her music and watched the gauges. Twenty more miles. Just twenty more miles. Very likely, she would trade the stress of this drive for a different kind of stress, but she was a lot better at wrangling wild nephews than she was at car repair. She'd take it.

With fifteen miles to go, her phone jangled, letting her know Mary was getting antsy, too.

"Hi, sis."

"Anne. Will you be here soon? My mother-in-law keeps handing the boys cookies, and I know they won't eat a bite of dinner tonight. I swear, family reunions are just an excuse to judge each other's parenting and sabotage it so there's more to judge."

Anne laughed. "You should put that on the back of the Musgrove family reunion t-shirts. I think it would be a big hit."

"But you are coming soon? I haven't been feeling well, and

it's all I can do to hold on until you get here. Everyone is out tramping around and opening the door every four seconds so there are more mosquitos inside than there are outside."

"How delightful. And yes, I'll be there in thirty minutes. Hopefully." As Anne slowed to a stop at a light, the whole steering column shook like a puppy with its favorite toy.

"What do you mean, 'hopefully'? Did you hit traffic?"

"Something like that." It was too hard to concentrate while on the phone with Mary, so Anne hung up and eased onto the highway, keeping her speed down. The cars behind her began to pass, one by one. She kept going until she limped her way up to the campground where her sister and all the family on Mary's husband's side were staying. The hood was emitting a strange smell, but she made it without being stranded next to a car-b-que. One win for the day.

Pulling her bags out of the back, she began dragging them towards the cabin where Mary was staying.

Carl, her brother-in-law, jogged out the door and met her halfway. "I'll take all of this. Mary is dying to see you. Go cheer her up a bit and make her forget about her convenient headache that shows up any time anyone asks her to do anything."

"I'll do my best." Anne kept hold of only her purse and ran up the steps. It was nice to be anticipated, wanted, knowing she had a place and purpose. She hadn't felt that in a long while. Not since... there was no use in letting her mind dwell there. She wouldn't let thoughts of Eric linger around like a ghost rattling chains in the attic of her mind. It had been so long, the boy she remembered was now a man—a wholly different person. Well, she assumed he was. Eric wasn't one for social media, and she wasn't one for stalking, so all she had was an idea of what he might look like now.

"Anne!" Mary got up from the couch where she'd been lying with a cold compress against her forehead. "I told them to stay inside, but Charlie and Colter ran right past me, and they could be half-way across the campground by now. Would you be a dear and round them up? Bribe them if you have to, but not with candy. Tell them I'll let them play on their tablets after dinner."

"Sure thing." The inside of the cabin was spacious, but it was noisy with pots and pans banging around in the kitchen while dinner was being prepped, and Mary's sisters-in-law laughing as they watched a movie in the den at full volume. Anne was happy to step back outside and have a look around. She tightened the strings of her sweatshirt and dug her hands in the pockets. The sun wouldn't set for another hour, but the temperature was already dropping.

She knew Mary was afraid every minute the boys were outside, picturing them poking a bear or running naked through a patch of poison ivy while being chased by a skunk. And knowing Charlie and Colter, those concerns were justified. Anne had never seen two boys so intent on mischief in her whole life.

She breathed in deep, inhaling the scent of cold clean air and pine needles—two things Beverly Hills didn't have. Well, that was a closing chapter on her life anyway. Maybe in the next one she would live up in the mountains.

"Charlie is a rotten potato head! His gas smells like an old lady's arm pit. Charlie Musgrove is afraid of girls!" Colter ran past, laughing his head off, followed by an angry little boy who didn't particularly like any of the insults being hurled at him so cheerfully.

Anne ran after them and caught Charlie around the middle before he could take the block of firewood he was holding to Colter's head.

"Hey now. Does Aunt Anne get any of these special insults? What do I smell like?"

Charlie whirled around and dropped his block of wood. He sniffed her, taking her question seriously. "Annie, you smell like apple candy. But it's just that spritzer stuff you wear. You don't actually have any apple candy, do you?"

Colter came charging at her and practically barreled her over with a hug. "Oh, she does smell like cinnamon apples. Are you going to play with us?"

"Yes, but first we have to go inside and wash our hands for dinner. I want to see. Who has the dirtiest hands?"

Both boys stuck out their hands, eager to win the dirtiest hands award.

Anne put a finger to her chin. "Wow, tough choice. They both have smidges of tree sap. Fingernails are properly caked with dirt. Okay, Charlie, yours are the dirtiest so I'll let you pick. Do you want to wash your hands first or second?"

"First!" He thought for a minute. "I mean, second. Colter has to wash first. Ha ha."

That started up an argument that lasted the entire time Anne spent herding them into the house and down the hall to the bathroom.

"Oh, Anne. You're here. Have you seen the neighbor yet?" Etta asked.

Lucy giggled from behind her. "He's dreamy. I've never seen so many muscles on one guy, but he's not bulky either. Like, the perfect blend of masculine grace."

Every time Anne had spent any length of time around Carl's beautiful blonde sisters, they had one topic on their mind, and it was always scoping for guys.

"I've been here for ten minutes. I haven't seen anyone not related to you." Anne squeezed her eyes shut as Colter chose that moment to flick his wet hands in her face. At least they were clean now.

Lucy shooed the boys down the hall. "Go see your mother, rug rats. We have important girl stuff to discuss."

Charlie wrinkled his nose, but he ran with Colter back to the living room. Based on the surprised squawk and follow-up lecture, they must have headed straight for Mary on the couch and jumped on her head.

"So," Etta said, squeezing Anne's hands. "Lucy and I went to say hello, very casually. And he's as nice as he is delicious to look at. His name is Eric Wentworth, he's totally single, and he's staying with his sister and brother-in-law for the whole week. Same as us."

"Eric Wentworth?" Anne whispered the words, hoping she'd somehow heard wrong. She thought about Eric all the time, but in the eight years since breaking up, they'd never run into each other. It was her hunch that he had gone out of his way to make sure of it.

"Yep. We invited him for dinner, but he said he already had plans for tonight. So, he's coming for breakfast tomorrow instead. You can meet him then. Lucy and I already have a bet about which of us will snag his attention, but maybe he'll like you best of all. He has a wounded-soul-in-need-of-repair look that is dying for someone quiet and understanding like you."

Lucy cocked her head, assessing Anne from head to toe. "Yeah, I mean, you still have it going on." She didn't sound very convincing.

Anne wasn't offended. It had been a long time since she'd had anything going on. At this very moment, she was in fleece pajama bottoms and sturdy sandals, paired with a faded sweatshirt. Travel wear. I've-given-up-finding-a-man wear.

Maybe it was a different Eric Wentworth. There was no need to panic or tear her wardrobe apart hoping she packed something nice. Besides, everything nice she owned was several years out of style. Anne's heart didn't listen to her pleas to stay calm. It pounded in her chest like a drum solo. She could fake being sick. Mary did it all the time. Nobody would blink an eye if Anne did it.

Mama Musgrove hollered that dinner was ready, and Lucy and Etta scrambled into the kitchen to beat the rush.

Anne stood frozen in place. No one here knew she had once been engaged to Eric Wentworth. Their relationship had been private and intense, full of moments stolen when he wasn't working, and she wasn't under the spotlight of her famous father. She had only been a sophomore in college. Eric had just finished his pilot training and required flight hours, and was excited to start flying commercially so he could pay off his substantial education debts. He'd be gone more than he'd be home, but they knew they could make it work. Until it all began to unravel.

Anne walked into the kitchen where happy chatter and chaos reigned. She was so not ready to see Eric again. It would probably be best if she snuck an apple to eat in her room in the morning. She'd come out when he was gone.

CHAPTER 2 ♥ SNEAKY BREAKFAST

Eric reached the crest of the hill and stopped to give Trapper some water, pouring it from his canteen into a collapsible dish. The dog's tail wagged in utter happiness at all the things he was getting to sniff and explore, but he was panting heavily.

"Time for a break, you menace." Eric rubbed the black lab's ears and was rewarded with a slobbery kiss.

He hadn't been around dogs much in the past decade. He moved too much and worked too much for that. Hanging around Trapper, his sister's dog, was like getting a trial run on what it would be like to have his own.

He pulled out his cell phone and checked the time. The two flirtatious girls from the family cabin next door had talked him into coming over for breakfast. Judging by the kids running through the yard and the sounds of laughter and teasing floating through the windows, it was a big friendly group. It shouldn't be too awkward.

He needed to head back and jump in the shower, though, if he wanted to make it in time. "Ready Trapper?"

The dog perked his ears up at his name. Eric set a bit of a faster pace on the downhill trail, and Trapper stayed beside him, only having to be coaxed occasionally to stop sniffing at a burrow or where another dog had marked its territory.

His sister and brother-in-law had hit the lake early, neither ever tiring of fishing or canoeing. Now that his brother-in-law had retired from the Air Force, the two of them enjoyed nothing more than spending time together talking and laughing. Theirs was a relationship he envied, but didn't quite know how to be a third wheel to.

Now that he was moving to be closer to them, he'd have to get used to it, or maybe find a significant other of his own. He hadn't had the best of luck in that department, with one significant heartache always coloring his attitude about trying again.

He thought of Etta and Lucy, the sisters he met yesterday. They struck him as kind and sweet, but also overly smiley and immature, even though they were probably only a few years younger than he was. Maybe he needed to acclimate himself to dating again, just like he had to acclimate to everything else as a recovering nomad. For too many years he'd focused on his career, not trusting any woman to make a long-distance relationship work. Now that he would be flying short jaunts for a private jet company out of San Francisco, he could have a social life again, whatever that might look like these days. He felt like an old man trapped in a young man's body.

Trapper picked up speed the closer they got to the cabin. Once inside, the dog headed straight for his food and water dishes before collapsing on his dog bed for a nap.

Eric checked on him after his shower, but he was still snoozing.

Using the mirror by the front door, Eric ran a nervous hand through his dark hair and then walked out, striding across the yard to the large cabin across the way.

He knocked on the front door, hearing the sound of excited little boy shouts and harried mom lectures on the other side. There was some shushing, and then Lucy, the shorter of the blonde girls, threw open the door and beamed at him.

Lucy reached out a hand and dragged him inside. "Come on in, Eric."

Etta, Lucy's sister, eager to be the next to greet him, ran up and gave him a tight hug, her hand running from the back of his neck to down his chest as she pulled away. She seemed to have a lot of experience in subtly attracting male attention while pretending to be innocently sweet—a dangerous combination. She smiled coyly at his reaction to her hug, which based on the temperature of his face, probably involved a lot of red.

"Good to see you again, Mr. and Mrs. Musgrove," he said, quickly turning to greet her parents. "Thank you for having me over for breakfast. I really appreciate it."

Lucy and Etta introduced him to the rest of the family, but it was clear many of them were focused on getting closer to the counter where the food line would start, and he was just the next in a revolving door of young men Lucy and Etta happened to bring home.

It was actually a relief. He wasn't looking for anything serious. Not on vacation anyway.

Mrs. Musgrove rang a large kitchen bell to get everyone's attention, and two little boys ran to look over the balcony from the top floor before tromping down the stairs. This cabin was twice the size of the one Eric and his sister and brother-in-law were staying in. It was more like a lodge, really, with a gigantic kitchen and rows of bedroom doors upstairs in knotty pine that matched the railing and banister.

Eric stayed out of the way until things calmed down and he could join the back of the food line.

After getting his breakfast, he sat down next to Lucy, at her insistence. On his other side were the two boys, who made quick work of dousing their pancakes in syrup and spreading the mess to their faces.

They didn't have much interest in him, but their conversation was fun to overhear. Apparently, they'd cornered a chipmunk earlier that morning, and according to them, almost had their faces torn off.

Their mother looked increasingly irritated the more they talked about it.

"Hey, where's Anne this morning?" Lucy asked. She turned to Eric. "She's the only one you haven't met yet. It's not like her to sleep in."

"Another sister?" Eric asked.

"Um, no. She's my sister-in-law's sister." She motioned to the mother of the two boys. Mary, if he remembered correctly.

"Anne said she wasn't feeling well," Etta said.

"Great. All we need is a raging case of the stomach flu making its way through the cabin." The mom of the boys sighed, as if it were already determined.

"Mary, don't be so doom and gloom. I bet she's worn out from getting those two monsters to bed last night. I could still hear them at eleven." Etta narrowed her eyes at her two nephews.

They smiled back with innocent, sticky faces.

"I swear I've met you before," Mary said, studying Eric. "But I can't place it. I grew up in Beverly Hills." She said the last part with a hint of pride. "And then I went to Pepperdine University and majored in journalism."

He hadn't been too far from either of those fancy places, but they might as well have been worlds apart. "I grew up in the crappy part of Encino, and as a pilot, I've been out of the country more than in for the past few years, so I don't think we've met."

She did look familiar, though. And her sister's name was Anne. His shirt collar suddenly felt tighter and his chest burned with warmth that radiated up his neck.

Mary pointed at him. "Okay, that makes sense. Anne dated some guy from Encino who wanted to be a pilot. She was going through this bad boy phase. Yes, I think it was you. Cocky and full of swagger, which Daddy hated. Anne Elliot. Do you remember her?"

Did he remember her? He wished he could forget her. What was he supposed to do now?

He about jumped out of his chair when the two boys, who had slunk away from the table, began pounding on one of the bedroom doors upstairs and hollering. "Anne! You promised you'd help us catch a chipmunk today. Open up!"

He watched Anne crack the door open and murmur

something to the boys, her voice filled with patient resignation. They pulled the door open wider and danced around her, tugging on her hands.

She looked beyond them, down to the rest of the family sitting at the table, and like magnets drawn to each other, their eyes met. It really was his Anne. Her hair was darker and longer than he remembered, but those luminous blue eyes were the same. She didn't look sick at all, just majorly embarrassed. She had obviously been hiding. From him. The longer he stared, the more her eyes flashed with a challenge in them, daring him to judge her for it. Then, having convinced the boys she'd be outside with them soon enough, she firmly shut the door.

***

Anne whirled around, looking for her shoes before remembering she had lined them up next to her suitcase. Her shallow, panicked breathing wasn't doing good things for her brain. She took a moment to breathe deeply before getting her shoes on and checking her hair and makeup in the mirror one last time. At least she'd had the sense not to try to look sick. With the Musgroves, you had to be prepared for just about anything, including being yanked out of your fake sick room.

Voices from the table still filtered up to her room. She could only hear bits and pieces, but Mary's voice tended to ring out, and Anne knew Eric's identity as her former 'bad boy' boyfriend had already been outed. So embarrassing. And such a light treatment of a situation that had been anything but a rebellious fling.

There was nothing to do but face everyone head on and downplay the significance of it all before the scrutiny ruined both their vacations. She couldn't hide in here forever and didn't want to.

Keeping her eyes trained on the stairs, she walked as casually as possible down to the breakfast table and pasted on a smile.

"Hi, Anne," Eric said, playing with his milk glass.

"Good to see you." She gave him an awkward wave and then moved to fill a plate with eggs and pancakes to warm up in the microwave. Eric Wentworth was here, five feet behind her, and just as handsome and full of 'masculine grace' as Lucy had described. She wished the years had been as good to her. Having a movie-star-turned-Botox-enthusiast for a father meant constant scrutiny of her own appearance. She knew very well she didn't have the curves or the glowing, youthful skin of the women at any of the Hollywood parties they used to attend.

Concentrating on the slowly-revolving plate in the microwave, she listened as Eric thanked everyone and excused himself to go back home. Good. It was his turn to hide.

Remembering she needed a fork, she turned and ran straight into Eric's hard chest. He held his plate up with one hand, the other one steadying her arm. They did that stupid dance where they both moved in the same direction and bumped into each other again. He smelled amazing, but she needed to get out of his way. The contact was bringing memories back in waves—ones she didn't want to examine right now.

"I'm so sorry." She stepped back and held still so he could move around her and put his plate in the sink, which he hurriedly did. She heard the water turn on and the sound of quick scrubbing.

"Are you feeling better?" Mama Musgrove asked, her eyes assessing Anne with concern.

"Yes. Nothing a little extra sleep couldn't fix."

"Come sit next to me, Anne," Mary said. "I want to hear about how Daddy and Lizzie are liking the new condo. Is the ocean view as fabulous as they say?"

"I haven't seen it yet, but I have pictures I can show you later. I'll take my food outside if that's okay. I promised the boys I'd go play with them." She smiled at Mary before stealing a glance at Eric. He'd been stalled on his way out by Etta, who was showing him her charm bracelet.

"Yes, those chipmunks won't capture themselves," he said, obviously still following the conversation despite his concentration on Etta's outstretched arm.

Anne's face heated. "Somehow my throw-away comment about searching for chipmunks turned into a planned hunt. I promise no chipmunks will be harmed in the attempt."

Her comment brought a small smile to his face, though he didn't look up at her.

Grabbing a fork from the drawer and her plate from the microwave, Anne hurried around him and stepped outside to find her nephews. Those two didn't care about beach front condos or ex-boyfriends. There would be no pesky questions out here. The air was still cold enough for her to see her breath, but it felt good; bracing, even. She could hear the boys hooting and hollering at least a hundred yards off, but couldn't quite place the direction with the sound bouncing around and echoing through the trees.

When the front door opened a few seconds later, Anne dashed around the side of the cabin and leaned against the log wall, listening for Eric's footsteps and letting her heartbeat slow back down. She took a bite of her eggs. The food would be inedible if she had to warm it up again, and she was hungry despite her frazzled nerves.

"This seems like an odd spot to eat your breakfast."

Anne about choked on her food. She glanced over to see Eric staring her down, his arms crossed.

She chewed quickly. "I'm trying to give you space."

"Well, we can't both give each other space or we'll both spend the week hiding in our rooms or skulking around corners. I don't want to do that, so let's talk about this." He looked down at her pancakes. "You don't have any syrup."

"It's fine." She took a bite of pancake to demonstrate. It was as dry and bland as she expected with nothing on it.

Eric shook his head. "Hang on." He dashed off towards his cabin, bounding over the fire pit and dodging camp chairs like he was winning an obstacle course race. He returned a minute later with a bottle of syrup, barely even out of breath.

"Tell me when," he said, swirling it over her pancakes.

"When. And, um, thank you."

"Come sit." He motioned toward the fire pit, and she followed him over, sinking into a camp chair. He took one a few feet away, filling the nylon throne like a king. He exuded strength and confidence, a command of the situation she wished she felt. He'd always been that way, to some extent. Being near him again brought those little things back: the way his hand felt in hers, the sound of his laugh, the taste of his kiss, the scent of his neck when they cuddled up on his faded couch watching movies together.

He laced his fingers together and leaned forward. "My sister and brother-in-law are treating this vacation like a second honeymoon, and I'm totally happy for them, but I've had my fill of solitude. Etta and Lucy asked me to take them on a hike later. Will that be a problem for you?"

"Why would that be a problem?" Anne fought the jealousy dragon coiling up inside her. "You three have fun."

"I assumed you'd want to come along. They made it sound like a family thing."

"Oh." Did she want to be there while Etta and Lucy worked their magic on him? They would be crazy not to try. "It will depend on whether Mary needs me to watch the boys."

"Of course. Family comes first." He looked away, probably well aware of the bitter note in his voice. "Just do whatever you would do if I wasn't here, and I'll do the same. Deal?"

"Deal."

He stood and walked back to his cabin, swinging the syrup bottle by its handle on one finger.

Anne felt a numbness creep over her. It was safer than giving in to regret, regret that she'd broken things off with the only man she'd ever loved, and regret that all the reasons for it now seemed stupid. She ate a few more bites and stared into the cold ashes of the fire pit until Charlie and Colter found her. They were a welcome distraction from her morose thoughts, and she happily joined them in their chipmunk hunt.

CHAPTER 3 ♥ ANY OTHER EXCUSES?

Eric heard his older sister's ringing laugh before the door handle turned and she and Adam came bursting into the cabin, carrying a cooler between them. Trapper hopped up from his dog bed to greet them, wagging his tail.

Adam grinned. "We had good luck at the lake today. We'll be eating rainbow trout for dinner."

"Sounds good," Eric said.

"What would you like with it?" Sophie asked. "Adam and I were going to head into town and stock up on groceries. Mashed potatoes or rice? And do you have an opinion on the side veggie? Maybe you should just come with us."

Eric set down the hiking magazine he was perusing. "I'm not picky. And actually, I'm going hiking with the neighbors in a bit. So, don't worry about me."

Sophie's eyes sparkled. "Is that right? When we met them yesterday, I noticed those two sisters couldn't keep their eyes off you. I take it breakfast went well, then?"

Eric's mind turned to thoughts of Anne hiding around the corner of the cabin with her breakfast plate. "Everyone was very friendly."

He wondered how much Sophie remembered about Anne. She hadn't met her, but his sister had been his confidant back then. She knew how much he had loved Anne, and the heartache he'd felt after leaving.

"Where are the Musgroves from again?" Sophie asked. "What are the chances you could turn a week-long camping fling into a real relationship? I won't judge you either way."

"I might," Adam said, giving his wife a dirty look. "I need him to focus on business, not long-distance relationships. I promised Captain Harville we'd work like dogs for him."

Sophie swatted her husband's chest. "You better be teasing me. The whole reason you two are getting into the private jet business is so you can be home more. Don't tell Eric he can't have a girlfriend."

"I'm just saying, she better be a special kind of distraction, otherwise dating can wait."

"Is that what I was?" Sophie asked, smiling up at her husband. "A special kind of distraction?"

Eric held up his hands to stop their flirtatious argument. They couldn't even fight without it turning into lovey-dovey eyes. "The family is from Van Nuys, but Etta and Lucy are sharing an apartment in San Francisco. So, if I did decide to date one of them, it wouldn't be long distance." It would be downright convenient, actually. He wished that wasn't the most compelling reason to consider either of them.

"Adam, I promise to pick someone within throwing distance of San Francisco Bay. Beyond that, I'm not picky. Any single woman between the ages of twenty-one and thirty-five can have me for the asking." *Anyone except Anne Elliot.*

Sophie frowned. "That sounds like the makings of a terrible relationship." She threw her arms out. "'Hello, ladies. I'm here, I'm desperate, and I'm not picky.' They'll be lining up in droves to fall at your feet, I'm sure."

"Always good for dating advice, Sophie. Thanks a lot."

He walked outside and across the yard, enjoying the crunch of pine needles under his feet. There was a Mercedes-Benz parked off to the side of the Musgrove's cabin. He'd noticed it yesterday, but hadn't given it much thought until now. It was exactly like the Mercedes Anne drove when they were dating, though it wasn't likely she still drove the same car. Her family wouldn't dare allow something around them to age, not even their vehicles.

And yet, Anne did look older. Usually women compensated by caking on the makeup, but not her. She looked softer now, more approachable. Strangely, it made her all the more attractive to him.

He shook off those thoughts. It didn't matter what he thought she looked like now. Anne was his past. Someone else would be his future; someone who wasn't so influenced by money and comfort they'd put it above true love.

***

Mary poked her head in Anne's doorway and knocked on the wood paneling. "It's time to go on the hike. You're coming with us, aren't you? My mother-in-law promised to watch the boys, and I think even you need an occasional break from them."

"I just got a break. Besides, how is she supposed to prepare lunch and take care of those two at the same time? I'll stay and help."

"We're taking picnic lunch sacks. They're already prepared. Any other excuses?" Mary's eyes narrowed. "Is it because Eric is coming? Don't think I didn't notice the way you two danced around each other this morning."

Anne sat up straighter. "We did not. It's just weird seeing him again, that's all."

"He thinks so, too. We were out there talking on the porch a few minutes ago, and Etta asked him about you. He said you looked so different he almost didn't recognize you."

Anne put a bookmark in her novel and slapped it on the dresser, irritated at how much the idle comment bothered her. Mary smiled, probably quite aware it wasn't exactly a compliment. Mary lived for drama, even the kind she had to stir up herself.

"He doesn't talk much, but you know Etta and Lucy. They just kept pestering him until he spilled his guts. He's an airline bus driver now, although from the way Etta and Lucy talk, you'd think it was the most glamourous job in the world. While Etta and Lucy were teasing him with Top Gun references and saying, 'This is your captain speaking,' I researched commercial pilots on my phone. The airline industry is having massive layoffs and pay cuts again. No wonder he's getting out."

"Getting out?" Anne asked. She shouldn't want to know, but she would have heard all this herself if she hadn't been hiding up here.

"Yep. His brother-in-law is an Air Force Lieutenant Colonel, newly retired, which is a lot more glamorous in my humble opinion, and yet they make about the same money. All that time and experience for nothing. Except now, they're flying for a private jet business together based out of San Francisco. It's not a bad idea. There are lots of rich people who would love a handsome guy like Eric telling them to come aboard. Slumming it with a jet pilot. That sounds exactly like something our dear sister Lizzie would do." Mary laughed.

The conversation was going so many places Anne wasn't comfortable with. She waved her hand in Mary's face. "Don't make fun of him. Do you have any idea how hard he had to work to get where he is? Pilot training is crazy expensive, and a lot of people can't hack it."

Mary rolled her eyes. "Hard work is so overrated. People should work smart. Like Carl. He turned his love for video games and hunting into the fastest-growing online game ever at age twenty. We're set for life. And he didn't have to go into massive debt to do it."

Depending on Mary's mood, she either complained endlessly about Carl and his man-boy hobbies or bragged on his accomplishments until everyone else left the room.

Anne pulled her hair back into a ponytail and picked up her jacket. "I'm surprised you're coming on the hike, Mary."

Mary looked offended. "I can hike." She looked down at her brand new joggers before straightening up. "Why should Etta and Lucy have all the fun?"

Anne followed her out and downstairs, glad the conversation had turned from whether Eric Wentworth could be called a success or not. It turned her stomach in knots just thinking about it, because years ago she might have taken comments like Mary's seriously. Calling a pilot an airline bus driver was just rude.

The rest of the hiking group was waiting for them outside— Carl, along with his dad, Charles, and of course, Eric, with Etta and Lucy attached to his sides. Eric had a black Labrador retriever with him on a leash.

"We're burning daylight," Carl complained. "Are you ready now, Mary?"

"I was retrieving Anne," Mary said.

Everyone turned to look at her. She saw disappointment in Eric's face. They had agreed not to avoid each other, and now she was drawing attention to it.

"Where are we going?" she asked.

"It's a short drive from here," Carl said. "We're hiking down near the lake. If you all don't mind squishing, we can fit in my Land Rover."

Mary frowned. "They'll get mud all over it when we get back in." She eyed the dog with Eric, but didn't say anything.

"Like our boys don't do that already. Have it detailed when we get back."

"All right."

The matter settled, Mary climbed into the passenger seat. Lucy and Etta got in next. Charles, their father, was a big man, and Anne didn't want him attempting to climb past the middle seats. She put a hand to his arm, murmuring, "I'm smaller. I'll get in back."

He nodded his gratitude.

It wasn't until Anne was in one of the third-row seats that she realized who that left sitting next to her. The Eric she knew wouldn't take the remaining middle seat after Anne had offered it to Charles. And he didn't. He and the dog, Trapper, climbed in back with Anne. Trapper bounded right onto Anne's lap before circling around to lick Eric's face. Finally, he collapsed, half on Anne and half on Eric.

"Sorry," Eric whispered, "I didn't know how the girls would do with the dog up with them, and the trunk's a little small. I thought he'd do better if he could see me."

Anne rubbed the dog's ears. "It's okay. He doesn't get car-sick, does he?"

Eric shrugged. "I'm not actually sure. He's my sister's dog."

Carl started up the SUV and they bounced down the gravel road out of the campground. Trapper's ears perked up, but otherwise he stayed still.

Concentrating on the dog meant Anne didn't have to think about Eric's shoulder against hers, or how the weight of the dog prevented her from putting more space between them.

"Did you find any chipmunks?" Eric asked, leaning his head closer so they could hear each other over the booming pop music Mary had immediately flipped on.

Anne caught the scent of his aftershave. She looked away from his perfectly kissable jawline and focused on the plush leather of the seat in front of her. "To be honest, I don't know the difference between a chipmunk and a squirrel. But we chased something bushy-tailed up a tree and ran around it brandishing our sticks."

"I had no idea you were so good with kids," he said.

"I didn't either until those two came along."

He stared into her eyes, and her breath caught, hating and loving his steady gaze. "How old are they?" he asked.

"Six and seven." She could see Eric calculating in his head. Mary met Carl soon after Anne's breakup with Eric. Carl had first been interested in Anne, but given her lack of interest, his attention soon turned to Mary. It was something they never talked about, as Carl had a good sense of self-preservation when it came to dealing with his wife's sensitive feelings.

"Have you been around kids much?" Anne asked.

"Not at all. Occasionally kids will want a tour of the cockpit with their parents, but that's it."

Lucy flipped around in her seat and smiled at the two of

them. "How's it going back here?"

Anne smiled back. "Good. Hey, will you lower your window? I think it'll help Trapper."

"Help him how?" Lucy asked.

"Help him not get carsick. It's a little stuffy back here."

Lucy quickly obeyed.

Trapper put his head up, and then his whole body, his paws scraping against Anne's jeans. He leaned forward as much as he could and hung his head out the window.

***

Anne had always been kind and accommodating, and clearly that was something time had not changed. It was one of the reasons her family took advantage of her so easily. Eric tried to remember that disheartening detail and forget about the way her golden skin darkened in the summer months, or the blue of her eyes, a color that had always reminded him of Emerald Bay at Lake Tahoe. He'd told her that once, and she had blushed and laughed, saying he complimented like a guy. What would she think if she knew he still had a screen saver of Emerald Bay State Park on his computer?

It was time to change it, along with so many other things; to stop living like someone with a broken heart and choose to move on. Being around her for the next few days would be good. Instead of this ghost haunting his past, Anne would be a real person who had moved on with her life.

Carl parked by the lake, and they all got out. Eric stretched his arms, laughing when Lucy ducked under one so she was in the perfect position for his arm to go around her. She was easy to flirt with. Not as blatant as Etta, and without the history that would always bog down any conversation with Anne.

They set off down the trail, and he was relieved when Anne fell in step with her sister and brother-in-law, leaving him several feet ahead with Etta and Lucy.

They wanted to know more about his life as a pilot, but their questions weren't about his travels so much as trivial things, like whether he ever met famous people, and whether a bird had ever hit the windshield while he was flying.

After a while, the conversation turned to Lucy and Etta's work at a tech company in San Francisco that recruited Etta straight out of college. Lucy had joined her there a year later. From the way they described it, the work was boring and repetitive, but paid extremely well. It also sounded like a lot of interoffice dating went on from the comments Lucy made now and again. Etta tried her best to subtly turn the conversation away each time, especially when Lucy mentioned a guy named Hayden.

"Why can't we talk about Hayden?" Lucy finally asked. "You two aren't exclusive."

Etta blushed to her roots. "Because..." She tilted her head in her brother's direction. "You know how Carl gets."

"Oh," Lucy said, giggling. She glanced at Eric. "Carl loves Hayden. Whenever those two are together, they talk endlessly about video game stuff. Carl is always telling Etta to give Hayden another chance, and she does. It's ridiculous." She turned to look at Etta. "You should just break it off for good already."

Etta glared at her sister. "That's easy for you to say when it's not your life we're talking about." She stomped off up ahead and caught up to her dad, who was taking the lead, brushing back tree limbs and bushes with his walking stick like he was leading a jungle safari.

"What about you, Lucy?" Eric asked. "Is there someone you're not exclusive with back home?" Eric said it more to be conversational, but realized how it might sound when he saw Lucy's earnest face. She surprised him though. She didn't turn it into a chance to flirt. Instead, she stared ahead with a determination he hadn't expected.

"I haven't found anyone worth my time yet. But when I do, I won't do this on-again, off-again and whether or not we should be exclusive nonsense. He's either right for me, or he's not. I won't be talked out of who I choose because if we're supposed to be together, what other choice is there? Am I right?"

"You're absolutely right." Eric couldn't help glancing back at Anne. She wasn't looking his way, but her hand was at her neck, and she looked pained.

He quickly turned back around and put his attention on Lucy. Part of him hoped Anne had heard, but he also didn't want to rub it in by staring at her.

He and Lucy continued to talk about work and somehow discovered they both spoke a little German, he because of several German co-pilots, and she because of a college roommate and the subsequent classes she took to learn more. It was embarrassing to find her memory of the language and her accent were much better than his. Maybe Lucy Musgrove was someone worth taking a second look at.

CHAPTER 4 ♥ THE WAY TO GET A MAN'S ATTENTION

About a mile into the hike, Anne knew she'd chosen the wrong shoes. They were hiking boots, but she didn't hike often, and the material rubbed against the back of her heel until the stinging made walking without a limp take all her concentration. Not that hiding it mattered. Mary and Carl had gotten into an argument about one of his aunts staying at the reunion and paid no attention to Anne at all.

From what Anne could surmise, Carl's shy aunt had tried on several occasions to talk to Mary, only to be ignored.

"I did talk to her," Mary insisted. "Is it my fault my interest in couponing and garage sales has a limit? I ran out of things to say. Coupons and garage sales are for people who obsess about every dollar and dime that passes through their hands. They're the reason I have to wait so long at the grocery store." She'd gotten louder with every word. Lucy giggled and glanced back before throwing Eric a long-suffering look.

Anne didn't have the mental energy to worry about the Elliot pride on display. She winced as another sharp pain hit the back of her foot. Continuing on, she blinked away the pain until she practically ran into Eric.

He stared her down with his arms crossed. "Sit," he

commanded, pointing to a nearby boulder.

She hobbled over to it. There was no use in pretending now. As soon as she had her shoe and sock off, he took one look and pulled out his cell phone, holding it up to see if he had service.

"One bar," he muttered.

"Who are you calling?" Anne asked in alarm.

He ignored her and tapped on a contact before putting the phone to his ear. "Sophie, where are you?"

Anne wanted to grab the phone before he asked for a favor on her behalf, but knowing how stubborn he could be, she knew any attempt to stop him would be thwarted. Trapper circled Eric while he talked on the phone, tangling him up in the leash.

Anne examined her heel, wishing it wasn't a painful disaster. The blister that formed earlier had popped, and the whole area around it looked angry. If she'd asked for moleskin in time, she wouldn't be holding everyone up now. So much for not drawing attention to herself. All she could do now was apply some antibiotic cream and a loose bandage over it. Carl offered to put her now-useless shoe and sock in his backpack.

Having given his sister directions to their location, Eric ended the call and looked at the group, assessing. "The paved trail is just down this hill, by the lake. If you don't mind cutting across to drop Anne there, my sister and brother-in-law are riding over on their four wheelers. Anyone else have a blister or a twisted ankle yet undisclosed?"

Nobody answered.

Anne wanted to glare at him, but she felt so indebted that she stared at the ground instead.

"Poor Anne," Etta said, taking the leash from Eric and coaxing Trapper into coming with her. "Let's cut through this brush down to the lake then." She followed her dad with his walking stick, and the rest of the pack fell in line until it was just Anne and Eric.

She stood quickly, using the toes of her bare foot to hobble through the brush. Unfortunately, since they were basically creating their own trail to cut across, her foot found a sharp rock or stick with almost every step.

She froze in discomfort when a particularly evil rock dug into the ball of her foot. Suddenly, big arms scooped her up, and she yelped in surprise. Eric held her against his chest, his deep, exasperated breaths landing against her neck.

"Put me down," she hissed. No one up ahead had turned around to look at them yet, but they would soon.

"Stop being a martyr. You're just making this harder."

"You rhymed," she said, automatically. She wished she hadn't, because she felt him stiffen and his hands tighten around her. *The Princess Bride* had been one of their favorite movies, and they'd often rhymed on purpose to annoy one another like Fezzik did to annoy Vizzini.

"Anne. Don't." His tone was soft, almost sounding defeated.

"Sorry." So much of today had been an uncomfortable trip down memory lane, although being carried in his arms was new.

Her shirt pulled up a little when he adjusted his hold, and the sensation of his warm fingers on her cold skin pulled all her attention there. It was exquisite torture.

"Eric, I promise I'm fine. Just put me down. I'm not as fragile as I look. Not that I look fragile. Never mind." Great, she was babbling.

He lowered her gently, and she adjusted her shirt, blushing when their eyes met. Her gaze flitted to his left hand, the one he was clenching and unclenching, the one that had been touching her skin.

He motioned for her to continue on, which she did, hobbling faster now that their destination was only a few yards away. They reached the paved trail and lined up along the side with everyone else to let a couple of mountain bikers by.

Lucy reclaimed her position by Eric's side, and the two chatted as if Anne wasn't there until his sister and brother-in-law pulled up on their four-wheelers five minutes later.

Anne began to apologize, but Eric's sister, Sophie, waved her off. "There's nothing Adam and I like more than a good rescue. Am I right, Adam?"

Her husband nodded. "Hop on back of one of these, and

we'll have you home in a second. Any other takers?"

Everyone else wanted to stay, which was a relief to Anne. She didn't want to disrupt their plans any more than she already had. She climbed on with Sophie, feeling a little awkward, but a lot relieved.

The two drivers were quiet until out of earshot of the group, and then Sophie hollered, "Looks like he's making progress. Which one of the sisters was standing there next to him looking like he was her knight in shining armor?"

Anne realized after a few seconds that Sophie was asking her. "That was Lucy," she called out.

"Eric is such a good catch. He deserves some happiness, and I think he's finally ready to try again. He was engaged once, you know."

Obviously, Sophie had no idea who Anne was, and Anne wasn't about to enlighten her if Eric hadn't.

"Are those your kids back at the cabin?" Sophie asked, turning her head slightly. "Your mother-in-law was having a good time with them by the campfire, though I think they ate ten toasted marshmallows each."

It would have been funnier if Anne wasn't so tense. "No, those are my sister's kids. She'll be thrilled to hear about the marshmallows."

They reached the main road that would lead them back to the cabins, and the two drivers picked up speed, thankfully rendering further conversation impossible.

Upon their return to the campground, Anne thanked them again and hurried inside to find a stressed out Mama Musgrove and two boys jumping from furniture piece to furniture piece in the living room. It was a miracle the side table lamps were still intact. The boys' faces were a mix of charcoal and sticky marshmallow remains.

"Charlie and Colter, get over here right now and let me see you," Anne said. "Who ate the most marshmallows? I want to see if I can tell by how sticky you are."

She gave it her best scientific study while arm wrestling them to the sink, where she scrubbed the sugar evidence off their faces. Then she gave them the job of finding all the shoes in the house and lining them up by the door. There would be some disgruntled shoe owners in the end, but Anne was tired, and it was all she could come up with at the moment.

Mama Musgrove sank into a chair, and Anne did the same.

"You're so good with them, Anne. I can't believe how nicely they sat while you looked at a dinosaur book with them last night. They absolutely run wild for the rest of us. The only way I can keep their attention is to bribe them with sweets. Otherwise, they run away from me, and I'm in no shape to chase them down the way you do."

"You did great. Maybe Mary won't find out about the marshmallows."

"Maybe. How was the hike?"

Anne laced her fingers together and rested them under her chin. "You didn't see me hobble in here? I had to be rescued by Eric's sister and brother-in-law because of a popped blister. It was humiliating." She lifted up her foot as evidence.

Mama Musgrove laughed. "I was so caught up in my own troubles, I didn't even notice you came in with only one shoe on. You poor thing. If you were more like Etta or Lucy, you'd have made that big, strapping boy from next door carry you. That's one way to get a man's attention, no doubt about it."

Anne blushed to her roots and excused herself to go clean up her foot.

***

Lucy pulled a granola bar out of her backpack and split it in two, handing half to Eric. She was thoughtful as well as intelligent. Another quality to add to the list.

She glanced up at the trees. "I love the smell of pines. Isn't it nice?"

"Yes, it sure is." Now that Anne had headed back to the cabin, Eric could actually breathe again.

A flock of cranes flew overhead, and they stopped to watch them.

"So, you and Etta live in San Francisco, and your parents in Van Nuys. What about everyone else?" Eric would not mention Anne by name, even though she was the one he was truly asking about. It was a stupid little mind game, but after scooping her up in his arms, he needed to know after this week he wouldn't run into her again.

Lucy swung her arms back and forth. "Mary and Carl aren't far from us. They live near Golden Gate Park, and the nanny takes the boys there nearly every day. The coupon-clipping aunt Mary was verbally abusing earlier lives in Arizona. That's where Mama's from. At the last reunion, there were a lot more Arizona cousins, but a lot couldn't make it this year."

A squirrel dashed across their path, completely distracting Lucy. Eric was afraid that was where the conversation would end, but Lucy turned back to him with a conspiratorial look and dropped her voice. "Anne is sort of in transition right now. Her father had to quickly sell their Beverly Hills Mansion before it went into foreclosure. He's up to his eyeballs in debt. Not that Mary ever brings up that part. All she talks about is her father's sweet little beachside condo in Malibu. I love her, but she's such a snob."

They both looked behind them, but Mary and Carl were several yards back, deep in their next argument. There was never any real heat in their words, but the spats were so frequent Eric wondered how the two had ever gotten together.

"Anyway," Lucy continued. "The Elliots used to rent the condo out to vacationers, but now they have to live there. Anne will probably join her dad after this week. The man hates to be alone. Her other sister, Lizzie, is there already." Lucy shrugged. "I couldn't do it. Personally, I couldn't wait to get away from home the second I graduated high school."

"Me too." Eric said, sharing a small smile with her.

They walked some more, and Eric couldn't help but notice how Lucy's arm would brush against his. Sometimes her fingers, too.

It was his cue to take her hand, or find opportunities to brush against her in return, but he hesitated. Holding Lucy's hand was taking them from friendship to a possible relationship, and he wasn't ready for that, no matter what he might have said to his sister. Besides, his thoughts were still on Anne. If she was living with her father, and at his beck and call, then nothing had changed. Anne hadn't changed. It filled him with a disappointment he wished he didn't feel. He wanted better for her and wished she wanted better for herself.

The trail sloped upward, and Lucy used Eric's hand and arm to balance as she climbed. The grateful, shining smile she tossed at him had his heart picking up speed, but not for the right reasons.

He was relieved when Etta joined them again, as if no argument between the sisters had ever parted them. Etta gleefully used Eric's limbs as support as well, and Lucy didn't seem the least bit bothered by it. He was overthinking this. Plain and simple. They were all friends, nothing more. Whatever he thought he'd seen in Lucy's eyes was merely flirtation on her part. Man, he was rusty. It was definitely time for a new relationship as soon as he was away from Anne again.

"Are we stopping for lunch soon?" Mary called out to them.

"As soon as we find a good spot, Mary," Eric assured her. He pulled out his map from his pocket and unfolded it. "We should reach the park benches in about a half-mile."

"Rain is in the forecast for tomorrow," Etta said with a sigh. "I say we drive somewhere before it hits. Any suggestions?"

"We could go see a movie," Lucy said.

Eric shook his head. "I can't go. My friend, Benneck, is coming tomorrow for a business meeting of sorts. I'll introduce you to him when you two get back."

"Is Benneck a pilot, too?" Etta asked, getting a coy, gleaming look in her eye. She really did have a thing for pilots. It was less flattering than it sounded.

"Etta." He gave her a warning glance. "I'm not sure how friendly he'll be, though heaven knows he could use more friends. His fiancée died of cancer last year, and he hasn't been the same since. I think flirting would only cause him stress, to be bluntly honest."

The two sisters were quiet for a moment.

"We'll be on our best behavior," Etta said. "Poor guy."

CHAPTER 5 ♥ NO MATCHMAKING NEEDED

The next day was nothing but rain, and therefore mud, and no one wanted to be outside except for Charlie and Colter. Finally, their dad took them out for a drive.

Mary parked herself at the foot of Anne's bed with a book, which was more of a hand accessory than reading material. She sighed and stared out at the rain hitting the window. "This weather is ruining all our plans. Lucy and Etta were supposed to plan a picnic in the meadow we found while out hiking. Instead, they ran off to see a movie and didn't invite anyone else. And there's a new Jeep parked over at Eric's place, and no one has come in or out of their cabin since."

Anne nodded absently. After the disastrous hike, she would have ducked out of picnic plans anyway. She did wish Mary would stop spying on the neighbors. Now, Anne was wondering who the owner of the Jeep could be, and it was absolutely none of her business.

"Which one do you think Eric likes better?" Mary asked. "Carl thinks it's Lucy, but I'm convinced Etta's a better fit."

Anne got out of the rocking chair in the corner, tired of feeling like some brooding old woman. All she needed to complete the look was one of her knitting projects and a lap blanket. "I think he should make up his mind already. Etta and

Lucy aren't the jealous types, but their competition for his attention will end in hurt feelings if he's not careful."

"And we'll be there to watch when it does." Mary looked almost gleeful about it. "You're still planning to stay in our guest house, right? The summer program told me in this totally passive-aggressive letter that Charlie and Colter aren't invited back this year. And their nanny is always studying for some exam or another and wants limited hours for the next few months. I'd fire her if the boys didn't like her so much. I don't care if you can't pay us rent like you planned. I still want you with us. The boys need you."

"I'll be working too, Mary. And yes, I'm still paying you rent." Anne thought of the natural history museum within walking distance of Mary's house. Even if her car really and truly was dead, Anne would be able to keep her new job.

"You still want to be a tour guide?" Mary snorted. "Whatever for? You and your love of dinosaurs. It's embarrassing."

It was embarrassing, but not for any of the reasons Mary thought. Anne had been so stupid in college. Paleontology was a study with no use until you had a master's degree, or better yet, a doctorate. It required time in the field, but Anne had traveled to practically nowhere. Dad had wanted her close, and since he had provided lavishly for everything she needed, she stayed.

Anne had laughably thought of herself as some kind of philanthropist back then, donating time and money to the museums and hobnobbing with the other donors, dipping her toe in the coursework but never really having a plan. And then the money ran out.

Asking for a job at the museum had been humbling, but also lifesaving. It gave her purpose. She was lucky to be able to transfer to the San Francisco museum and not have to start over again. One way or another, she was clawing her way to independence, however poor that made her.

Something Mary had said earlier caught hold, and Anne whirled around. "You said we'd be there to see it, when Eric chooses one of them. What did you mean?"

Mary shrugged. "I mean Etta and Lucy are at our house

constantly, and therefore, so are all their friends. We have a theater room, a gourmet kitchen, and a game room. I know those girls think I'm a total snob, but it's never stopped them from taking advantage of all our nice things. If they drag Eric along, so much the better. He's not nearly as bad as some of the other idiots they bring to our house."

Anne struggled with knowing she might have to continue to see Eric. But the alternatives were dire. Rent was super high in San Francisco. She couldn't afford to live anywhere else yet. She had planned to save up for her own place while living at Mary's.

"Mary, there may be a hitch in my plan to follow you back to San Francisco in my car. It was rattling the whole way here."

Mary sighed. "I know you don't want to ask Daddy for something else, but how unfair is it that Lizzie is driving a brand-new BMW while you still have that piece of junk? Don't worry. We'll get it towed, and you can sit in back with us and entertain Colter and Charlie. Win-win."

An eight-hour drive sitting between those two. It was only what Anne deserved if she let Mary pay for her car to be towed. "I'll drive into the city tomorrow and have someone look at it first and see what's wrong with it."

"That sounds like a long, boring day," Mary said, making a face. "Plus, Carl will insist on going with you, and I'll be left with the boys."

"Carl doesn't have to go with me."

Mary dropped her book and pressed her nose to the window. "Oh, finally. Eric's walking over here, and he has someone with him. A man. He's taller than Eric, and just as good looking. That should make Etta and Lucy practically pee themselves."

"It's not Eric's brother-in-law, Adam?" Anne asked.

"Nope."

Anne paced around the room, unsure what to do. If she had to stay cooped up in this bedroom much longer she'd scream, but making small talk with Eric and his friend would be just as bad. A greasy car repair shop was sounding better and better. She wished she had braved the mud and bad weather today and not wasted away the afternoon.

Mary ducked into the adjoining bathroom and smoothed her hair. "Let's go see what they want. And don't even think about hiding up here. Even you can't be that anti-social. I won't allow it."

***

Benneck gripped Eric's arm as Eric went to knock.

"Do I really need to meet your vacation neighbors?" Benneck asked. "Isn't the whole point of a tranquil vacation in the woods to be like Walden and avoid people and just enjoy nature?"

"If you start quoting Henry David Thoreau again, I swear I'll leave you here alone with the Musgroves like a gift on their doorstep. Not that it would be a bad thing. They're very nice people."

"I'm sure they're very nice. I'd just rather not have the stress of conversation and smiling and all that."

"Benneck, we just talked about this with Adam. Our jobs are all about socializing and making people feel welcome, not just flying them places. Consider this practice. Which you need."

Eric felt only a small twinge of guilt. Benneck needed someone to stop coddling him. He'd had too much of that, to the point where he expected it from everyone. Benneck used to be the life of a party. Now he acted like socializing was a punishment.

Benneck gestured toward the door. They'd been standing in front of it without knocking for more than a minute now.

"Oh, I can knock now?" Eric asked.

Benneck slugged him in the arm. Hard.

Eric laughed and rubbed the sore spot. "Okay, okay. Truce." He knocked on the door, and they waited several seconds before Etta and Lucy answered together, both giving off the heavy fragrance of hair product and perfume mixed with a whiff of movie theater popcorn.

"Your timing is perfect. We just got back," Etta said, motioning for them to come inside.

"How was the movie?" Eric asked.

Lucy linked her arm through his. "It was stupid, but you probably would have loved it. Lots of explosions and beautiful women kicking butt, and very little plot."

"Yes, that sounds exactly like Eric's type of movie." Benneck reached out a hand, and Lucy shook it enthusiastically.

"You must be Benneck," Lucy said, beaming at him. She moved aside so Etta could introduce herself. The fact that neither tried to hug the guy or touch his muscles showed how well the two sisters had taken Eric's warning to heart.

"It's nice to finally meet you," Lucy said. "Eric had such nice things to say about you."

"I highly doubt that. Tell me what he really said."

Lucy's blinked back at Benneck in surprise. She didn't know him well enough to decipher if he was serious or joking.

Etta, always bold, just shrugged. "He said you're sad right now and not to flirt with you."

Benneck sniffed. "Accurate. And now we don't have to tiptoe around the subject. All the better."

Eric glanced around the rest of the great room, noticing for the first time that Mary was sitting at the kitchen table listening to every word, and Anne was curled up in the corner with a book.

It was a sight Eric remembered very well from years ago, except now Anne wore reading glasses, giving her a hot librarian look he immediately wished hadn't occurred to him.

"Benneck, stop trying to make everyone feel uncomfortable. Let's play cards or something. I see a stack of decks over there by the TV." Eric retrieved a couple decks of cards and set them on the kitchen table across from Mary. "Would you like to play cards with us?" he asked her.

Mary sighed. "Okay. It's not like I have anything better to do."

"Mary," Anne murmured, sounding embarrassed. It was the first indication she had been paying attention at all.

Lucy looked at Mary with disgust before turning to Anne. "Are you going to play, Anne?"

Anne glanced up from her book for the first time and took in the group. "What are you playing?"

"Spoons." Eric walked to the kitchen and checked several drawers until he found the right one. "Where are your parents, Lucy?"

"With my aunt and uncle. And Carl is out mud bogging with the boys. So we only need four spoons. Well, five if Anne is playing."

As Eric suspected she would, Anne made an excuse not to play. He was both relieved and disappointed.

Etta and Lucy claimed the spots on either side of him at the table, and Benneck sat next to Mary and introduced himself. She didn't remember how to play, so Benneck explained the rules while Eric made sure he had a full deck before shuffling and dealing out the cards.

Mary lost the first three rounds and grew increasingly frustrated at ending up without a spoon. It didn't help that Lucy giggled every time Mary came in dead last.

"Should we play something else?" Eric asked. He drew all the cards back in front of him and took his time jogging and shuffling them.

"We should play two truths and a lie," Mary suggested, looking over at Benneck. "That way we can find out stuff about each other."

As if she could trick Benneck into revealing something he didn't want to. Mary was not the type who invited confidences.

"I'll go first," Etta said. "I've already thought of my three. I hate the smell of bacon. I once got in a fight with a clown on Halloween. Oh, and I once had a hamster named Nancy." She poked Lucy. "You can't say anything since you already know."

Eric exchanged glances with Benneck before answering. "I'm hoping the clown one is true. I'll say you didn't have a hamster named Nancy."

"She loves bacon," Mary said. "I think that one's the lie. She ate five pieces yesterday morning along with her pancakes and eggs."

Etta turned her back to Mary and leaned toward Benneck. "What about you, Benneck? Which one do you think is the lie?"

He crossed his fingers, lacing them under his chin. "I think you made up the clown one. Who's correct?"

Etta smiled. "I do love bacon but I hate the smell of it in my hair and clothes from cooking it. My hamster's name was Maggie. Which means Eric got it right. Congratulations. The clown I got in a fight with was my brother, Carl. He kept scaring me with his stupid scary makeup and his bright orange curly wig, so I punched him right in the nose, and it started bleeding. We both got in trouble and had to go to bed early."

Mary's mouth dropped open. "I thought you and Carl always got along."

Etta shrugged. "We usually did. He just happened to be a twelve-year-old boy at the time, and they can't help themselves. They're so annoying age at that age. Am I right, you two?"

Eric smiled. "You're not wrong."

"You should go next," Benneck said, nudging Eric with his elbow.

"Me?" Eric glanced around. "Okay, sure." He thought for a moment, but the ideas that came to him had Anne attached to them, or involved things they'd once laughed about. He tried again, clearing his mind of all Anne-related thoughts. "I once made an emergency landing in Turkey during a dust storm. I talk in my sleep. And I hate jelly beans."

"Everyone hates jelly beans," Mary declared. "They're awful. Especially the purple ones."

"I think the emergency landing one is a lie," Lucy said, studying him.

"Me too." Etta smiled at him, lacing her fingers under her chin. "I bet you do talk in your sleep. But how do you know? Who's in the bed with you?"

"Etta," Lucy said, slapping her sister's arm.

One quick glance confirmed Anne was, indeed, listening in. He wasn't sure why that mattered, but having her in the room was enough to constantly distract him. Eric turned back to Etta.

"No one is in my bed except me. But my mom said I talked in my sleep a lot growing up. Maybe I don't anymore. I haven't lived at home since I was eighteen."

"He still talks in his sleep," Benneck said with a laugh. "We've had to share hotel rooms for work. I'd forgotten about that fun little habit of his."

"And what does he say?" Etta asked, leaning forward.

"All gibberish. But in an intense voice. Like he's having an argument with someone."

Mary tapped the table. "You're not supposed to reveal the answers until we've all guessed. So, which one is the lie, then?"

Eric put his hands out. "The emergency landing was actually in Greece, and one of Tom Hanks' sons was on board."

That started a whirlwind of questions from the girls about celebrities, which morphed into a discussion of the hottest actors in Hollywood and who they most wished would show up in their hot tub on the back porch.

Eric slumped back in his chair. "I think this conversation is better left for girls' night. I'm ready to call it a night." Although finding out their lodge had a hot tub on its back porch was interesting news. His did too, but he wasn't interested in going alone or sharing it with his sister and brother-in-law.

"We'll stop. Stay." Lucy gave him her most pleading, innocent look.

Eric caved, but Benneck slid his chair out, clearly unmoved. "I'm joining the book club over here." He headed over to the couch where Anne was sitting, despite continuing protests from Mary, Etta, and Lucy for him to come back. Lucky dog.

Eric wished he could do the same, and not just because he was tired of talking about celebrities.

***

Eric's friend was very good-looking, with his large blue eyes, tan complexion, and sandy-blond hair, but he had an air of not caring much about his appearance, or much about anything that had to do with expectations. She gave him a small smile when he sat down next to her on the couch. He was obviously curious about her, and she was curious as to why that would be.

"I'm Benneck. And you are?"

"Anne." She set her book off to the side and shook his hand.

"So, who are you avoiding?" Benneck quietly asked.

"I was just reading."

He crossed his arms. "Reading and holding a book up in front of your face are not the same thing. But I'm not going to quiz you, because no doubt you would quote that entire book to me in an attempt to cover up whatever else is going on. Just know I'm on to you. Well, vaguely on to you. I guess we'll be two introverts hiding from the world over here."

"You're not an introvert," Anne said with a small smile. "You introduced yourself to me without being compelled, and now you're acting like we're already friends."

"Aren't we? And I didn't say I was an introvert, only that it would be our cover story."

"So, what tragic secret has you in hiding?" Anne asked. She said it in jest, but when his face tightened she wished she could take the words back. Instinctively she knew if she apologized, he would clam up harder than an oyster guarding its pearl. She smiled instead. "Nope, don't tell me your secret. We'll be tragically mysterious together."

He immediately relaxed back against the couch. "Good plan. Mysteriously unhappy is much better than being a killjoy. That's usually my role. Just ask Eric."

"Of course he would say that about you." Eric had always been a buck-up-and-take-it-like-a-man kind of guy.

"Ouch, that hurts, woman. I mean, I am a buzzkill most of the time, but you don't have to agree with him."

Anne laughed, realizing Benneck had no idea she had been referring to Eric's personality with her comment and not Benneck's. But she wasn't about to fess up to knowing Eric, despite her slip of the tongue. "It's just, you two seem like the type who like to tease each other."

"That's true. So, let's see this book of yours. Is it any good?" He held out his hand for it.

Anne picked up her book and handed it to him. His eyes widened as he took in the glossy black cover with a ring of fire in the middle.

"The Sorcerer's Mask of Freedom?"

"Were you expecting a romance book?" she asked.

"I'm not sure what I was expecting. Is this fantasy?"

"Yes."

"Hmm. I'm usually a die-hard sci-fi kind of reader. I'm not really into elves or mages or wizards and all that."

"Well, this is more of a political thriller with magical elements. The guild lives alongside humans, influencing things without their knowledge." She watched Benneck as she spoke, waiting for his eyes to glaze over in that tell-tale sign the conversation had reached nerd overload, but he looked intrigued. That was new. No one in her family understood her reading tastes.

He asked some more questions, about whether the book was part of a series and what else she liked to read. He was fun to talk to, but Anne couldn't help glancing behind him occasionally to the other group, keeping tabs on things, though she never let her eyes lock with Eric's.

Eric seemed to be doing the same thing, and he looked torn, as though he couldn't stand that Anne was deep in conversation with Benneck, but was pleased by it too. It was so strange.

"I can set you up with him," Benneck said, smiling at her in a knowing way.

"Oh." Anne looked down at the couch. "No, I wasn't... I was just checking on Etta. She can be a little forward without meaning to be." Etta's laugh pealed out as evidence.

"Whatever you say. I don't mind. I plan to be alone the rest of my life, but that doesn't mean I can't dabble in a little matchmaking."

Benneck planned to be alone the rest of his life? The guy did like to throw maudlin statements out there just to see how people would react. Well, he wouldn't get a reaction out of her, at least not about that part.

"No matchmaking needed. I promise."

"Why not? Eric's a good guy."

"Just, no."

He raised an eyebrow. "Okay, I promise. Subject dropped. Let's try to out-nerd each other instead. I'll say something about myself that reveals my inner nerd, and then you have to one-up it."

Anne shrugged. "Okay, why not?"

"My favorite movie is Galaxy Quest."

Anne thought for a minute. "I like to knit sweaters for my sister's hairless cat."

Benneck snorted, covered his mouth, and then held up a hand while he tried to compose himself. "We're supposed to start out slow, Anne. How am I supposed to one-up that? Also, do you have pictures?"

Anne laughed. "I have lots of pictures. My sister, Lizzie, hates that I do this because she buys her cat designer sweaters and mine are lumpy and ugly and in her words 'not worthy of Beauregard.'"

"There are designer sweaters for cats? And also the cat's name is Beauregard?"

"Shh." Their laughter was drawing everyone's attention. "Be quieter. Mary will tattle on me to Lizzie."

"Mary's your sister?" Benneck asked, glancing back and forth between Mary at the table and Anne. "Okay, I sort of see the resemblance."

Though Anne and Mary were very different in personality, they shared the same mouse-brown hair and high cheekbones. Lizzie had been the one to get their mother's blonde hair and curvy figure, something she often liked to point out.

"Here is Beauregard." Anne pulled out her phone and scrolled back to the latest pictures she had taken of the cat before leaving for Big Bear Lake. She sort of missed him hanging out in her room, looking like he was silently judging her.

Benneck took one look at him and couldn't stop laughing.

"He's so ugly, and yet I bet he cost a fortune."

"Yes. To both of those."

"How much was he?" Benneck asked.

"I'm not saying. Besides, aren't you supposed to one-up me now?"

He rolled his shoulders back. "Let me think. Okay, I once did a dance routine with my sister to an NSYNC song in a talent show."

Anne tilted her head. "Okay, but how old were you?"

"Eight."

"Nope, that's adorable. It doesn't count. What else do you have?"

He sighed. "I didn't want to have to admit this one. I sing 'Twinkle, Twinkle, Little Star' in my head while washing my hands to make sure I do it long enough."

Anne smiled big. "I do, too. Except I recite 'Row, Row, Row Your Boat' twice."

"You do not." He looked perturbed. "You can't be serious."

"Completely serious. But can you name the three periods of the Mesozoic Era? And do you own a triceratops costume?"

"Anne!" Benneck gripped his hair. "I surrender. You win, nerd."

CHAPTER 6 ♥ NOT EVEN THE DOG WAS THERE TO JUDGE HIS LIFE CHOICES

"Did you have a good time?" Eric asked Benneck on their walk back to the cabin. The stars overhead were putting on a spectacular light show, and he stopped to stare.

"You sound like you wish I hadn't. Jealous maybe?"

"Of your nerd game?" Eric shook his head. Was Eric jealous of Benneck for getting to spend time with Anne? Absolutely not. Benneck could laugh about her pretentious family with her because he hadn't been burned by any of them.

But maybe Eric was a little jealous that Anne brought out the old Benneck in one sitting. Not that she did it on purpose. She was just this genuine, lovable person, and Benneck had recognized it in her. She had no ulterior motives, no secrets or promises to extract from him. It was exactly the type of friendship Benneck needed right now.

Eric had to stop analyzing it. It was making him grumpy. Hearing Anne's laugh and knowing he wasn't the one causing it, okay, yeah, maybe it had made him a little wistful. But not jealous.

They trekked through the oozing mud back to their cabin, left their boots by the front door, and ate dinner with Sophie and Adam. The food was great, the conversation better, but Eric watched Benneck slowly retreat back to his usual melancholy self, despite their best efforts. Maybe it was Sophie and Adam with their constant love fest. Eric was getting used to it, but Benneck had only just met them. They were a living emblem of the perfect future taken from him.

His friend stayed up late watching sad war movies and drinking Mountain Dew.

When Eric awoke the next morning, Benneck was in the same position on the couch in front of the TV, except his head had lolled back and he was snoring loudly. Eric took a ten second video to torture him with later. Then, he ate a quick bowl of cereal and went outside, planning to walk around and enjoy the quiet, Walden-style. Benneck would be so proud.

He kept to higher ground, avoiding the few mud puddles left from yesterday, until he reached the tree line. The Musgrove lodge door creaked open, and he stepped behind a tree, not sure if he wanted the company. It depended on who it was.

His heart rate kicked up when he saw Anne step onto the porch, lifting the hood of her jacket up over her hair like she was about to enter a covert spy operation. Apparently, she was trying to avoid people this morning, too. She closed the screen door behind her with careful slowness before easing herself down the front steps. Once in the clear, she jogged over to the older Mercedes, parked not too far from where he was hiding.

Curiosity got the better of him, and he stepped out from behind the tree for a better look. A twig snapped under his foot, causing Anne to stop short and peer into the trees. She gave a little scream when she saw Eric watching her.

"You scared me," she said, clutching her chest. The hood of her jacket fell back, revealing her pink ears and cheeks, reddened from the cold.

"Where are you going?" he asked, looking at the car. It really was the same one from eight years before.

"Just out for a drive." She got in and shut the door. He saw her watching him in her rearview mirror, and when he didn't move, she finally started up the car, which immediately began to shake. She backed up, and a rhythmic clunking noise started up.

Eric walked around and stepped in front of her car, hoping she wouldn't try to drive around him or engage him in a stubborn game of chicken. Whatever was going on with her car would get a lot more expensive by the mile with all that shaking.

She rolled her window down and leaned out. "Eric, let it be. I got this. The car just needs to warm up." The pleading look in her eyes almost had him giving in. But the thought of her stranded somewhere would be worse than hurting her pride.

The door to his cabin creaked open and Benneck stepped outside in his pajama pants and flip flops, squinting as he surveyed the situation. "There's a good chance the motor mounts are bad. Let's hope it's not anything worse. Turn it off and let me have a look."

Anne's shoulders lifted and dropped with the big sigh she let out. But she turned off her car and popped the hood release under the dash. She got out, hugging herself and glancing around like she wanted to be anywhere but there with them and her sick car.

"I won't hurt your car, Anne. Stop looking at me like that," Benneck said as he walked over.

"It's not that. I just don't want to bother you with this. I was going to take it to an auto shop in town."

So much for her story about going for a drive.

Benneck began fiddling under the hood before going over to his truck to dig around in his tool chest.

Anne paced nearby, passing back and forth in front of Eric until he reached out instinctively and touched her arm. She stopped and looked at him, her despondent look nearly spearing Eric's heart. Her hair was falling out of a messy bun, wisps of flyaway pieces floating in the breeze. He resisted the urge to smooth it out.

"Benneck can fix just about anything. And he doesn't mind. It gives him something to obsess about."

"You have to make him accept payment then."

Eric shrugged. "That's your fight."

Benneck wiped his hands off on a rag and walked over. "So, definitely the motor mounts. We should probably replace the shocks while we're at it. Let me make a few calls and see if anyone has the parts in stock." He slipped his phone out of his back pocket and walked to the passenger side, pulling open the glove box and checking the make and model number from her insurance information. "Do a search, Eric, while I call the nearest Auto Zone. See what other options we have for getting parts."

"Sure."

The door to the lodge creaked open, and Eric and Anne turned to see who would shortly be joining them. Lucy came out, looking a lot more put together than Anne, both in terms of dress and temperament. She yawned and stretched, tossing her loose curls back off the shoulder of her baby blue sweater, not a care in the world.

"What's going on out here?" she asked, leaning over to look under the open hood of Anne's car.

"Benneck's investigating the cause of a little vibration problem I'm having. It's no big deal." Anne glanced at Eric, warning him not to say anything else. And there wasn't much to tell yet anyway. Not until they found parts. He went back to searching on his phone for local auto part stores.

Benneck motioned for Anne to join him, and the two of them put their heads together to listen to whoever was on the other end of the phone call. Benneck put his arm around her shoulder and squeezed, whispering something.

Not for the first time, Eric wondered if the two of them could fall for each other, and if they'd be good together. Benneck deserved some happiness, and if he found it in Anne... Eric took a bracing breath. It would be fine. This was better for everyone.

"Hey, you." Lucy sidled over and rested her head on Eric's shoulder as she looked down at his phone. "So, what's the big adventure for today?"

"Don't know yet. Did you and Etta have something in mind?"

"Actually, about that. Etta's on the phone with Hayden. They're officially back on again, and he's driving up here. I was thinking maybe you and I could go on our own hike. Maybe have a picnic."

"Uh-huh." Eric glanced from his phone to Lucy, pulling his thoughts from the map he was studying to what Lucy had just said. It wasn't until he saw her hopeful expression that it all sank in. Etta was no longer single, and apparently Lucy was interested in him after all. It was way too much pairing off for one morning, and Eric wasn't sure how he felt about any of it.

Lucy gave his bicep a small squeeze. "But if Benneck needs your help here..."

"I'm not much of a car guy, but I want to be here if he needs me." Eric glanced over at Anne, but she was watching Benneck finish up his phone call, looking resigned to the situation.

Benneck put his phone away. "I found a NAPA auto parts not too far from here and they have what I need in stock. Anne and I can go pick up parts and then we'll come back here and get to work. Me and my assistant grease monkey." He poked Anne's side, coaxing a small smile out of her.

"Eric is free then?" Lucy asked. From the way she was smiling, it seemed she, too, assumed Anne and Benneck might want some alone time. Eric had been hoping that had all been in his head.

Benneck glanced at Eric and shrugged. "I should be fine. I need to find a piece of plywood to brace between my car jack and her engine block, but we'll pick that up at the hardware store." He rubbed his hands together. "This will be fun."

***

Anne knelt by her car, watching Benneck work and trying not to think about Eric and Lucy out picnicking alone together.

She should have seen this coming. She should have claimed dibs on her old boyfriend from the start, even if the dibs were solely, he-once-was-mine-so-none-of-you-can-have-him. Girls could do that. It's what any of the others would have done. But

Anne hadn't said anything, and Lucy and Etta hadn't asked for permission. They were too smart for that.

"Can I hand him a wrench now?" Charlie asked, fidgeting in his lawn chair. The two boys were enthralled with the whole car repair process, but they hadn't been allowed to help with anything for several minutes. The less Benneck talked, the more Anne knew he was trying to concentrate, and he hadn't said anything beyond grunts for a while. The poor man was working in the dirt without the wheeled roller thing most mechanics used to go back and forth under cars.

Anne would owe him for life. She had insisted on paying for all the parts and materials they bought, including a few tools he didn't have with him in his truck, but the labor was all him. They'd laughed about it on the way home, with Benneck teasing her on what she had to offer in exchange for his help. He had already claimed two dozen homemade peanut butter cookies, a crocheted hot pad in his favorite colors, unlimited pictures of Beauregard the cat until the end of time, and a lecture on the family tree of ancient birds.

"Okay, you two." Anne took a dirty little boy hand in each of hers and lifted Charlie and Colter to their feet. "I happen to owe Benneck a batch of peanut butter cookies. You want to help me make them?"

Colter shrugged. "Nah, I'd rather stay out here and watch."

Unfortunately, Charlie agreed. The two of them had already eaten their way through a bag of mini candy bars, so the lure of sugar wasn't strong enough to sway them inside.

Anne glanced around, trying to think of something they could do out here. "What if we do some car maintenance of our own?"

That had them excited. Anne led them into the lodge for supplies. Quickly realizing any rags she took from the place would be destroyed, she grabbed an old t-shirt from her room instead. Charlie and Colter gaped at her when she cut it in half with a pair of kitchen scissors.

"This is not permission to cut up clothes, you two. I catch you doing that and you're both dead. Got it?"

They nodded solemnly.

She handed them a piece of t-shirt and grabbed a bucket from under the sink and the dish soap. "Let's go shine up my car's tires. What do you say?"

For a moment she was afraid they'd balk at the idea, but they ran outside eagerly. She filled the bucket halfway with water at the spigot on the side of the lodge and squirted in a little soap before letting the boys dip their rags in it.

She felt a little bit of shame when Charlie wiped his rag around the rim of her tire and revealed the shiny silver below the grime. Car washes were an expense she rarely splurged on these days. Two boys with makeshift rags did not exactly replace the real thing. After several minutes, they moved from wiping grime off the tire rims to spreading it around to the other surfaces of her car in their attempts to clean it. But they were so earnest in their efforts, she couldn't bear to stop them.

"You're a genuine Mary Poppins, Anne." Benneck grinned at her as he came out to rummage around in the tool bed of his truck. "You even look like you've been hanging out with a gang of chimney sweeps."

Charlie and Colter definitely fit the part, with tire grease as much on their hands and arms as on their rags. Mary would have a fit when she saw their clothes.

Benneck stretched out his back and groaned before sliding back under her car. Why he was doing all this for her was still a mystery. Some was goodwill, some was budding friendship, but there was a single-minded focus there too, one that covered up whatever it was he didn't want to dwell on.

The crunch of car tires alerted Anne to someone driving into the campground. She peeked around her car and took a deep breath. Eric and Lucy were back.

Lucy's window was down, her hand windsurfing in a carefree way that made Anne sigh. They must have had an excellent time. She forced her mind not to dwell on the specifics of what that might look like. Unbidden, an old memory of resting her head in Eric's lap as they sat under a tree returned, clear and sharp. His fingers had slowly drifted through her hair while they talked about their future together. A future that never came to be. Anne pulled herself back to the present and away from such gloomy thoughts.

Lucy got out first and came to stand next to Anne, surveying the dirty swipe marks left to dry on the side of her car. The boys were slapping each other with their rags now, stopping now and then to drag them through the dirt to get them extra disgusting.

"Oh, Anne. We should have stayed to help you. Dare I ask where Mary is?"

"She and Etta went to the grocery store. They planned to prepare a special dinner in honor of Hayden coming tonight. We're okay here. At least I am. How goes it, Benneck?"

"A few more minutes." It was the same answer he'd given the little boys whenever they'd asked. His few minutes estimate could very well be a few more hours. There was no way to tell.

Eric walked over, dodging the two little boys when they swept past him brandishing their mud-covered rags above their heads. His eyes took in Anne, lingering on her face longer than she felt comfortable with. She felt measured, and wasn't sure if he found her lacking or not.

He finally looked away and knelt down to peer in at Benneck. "What can I do?"

"Right now? I just need quiet. Take the two hellions elsewhere, and I'll finish this up in no time."

"Will do."

Well, why hadn't Benneck just told her that? Men. They were so direct with each other. Anne wished they didn't think women couldn't take it if they talked the same way with them.

"Colter, stop this instant." Lucy grabbed for the kid on his next lap around the car, but he easily squirmed out of her grasp. In the effort, his rag flew up and whapped her in the chest, leaving a line of mud across her beautiful blue sweater.

She whimpered and wiped at the mess, only succeeding in smearing it around.

"I got this, Lucy. Go on in and find their bath stuff, will you?" Anne nodded encouragingly. "I'll bring them in soon."

Lucy didn't need more coaxing than that. Putting on a brave

smile, she glanced back at Eric one last time before heading inside.

"Whose idea was it to give them mud weapons?" Eric murmured in her ear. He'd moved closer to Anne than she'd realized, close enough for her to catch the scent of his cologne despite the fact that she smelled like car parts.

"They started out as cleaning rags."

"Mmm hmm. I see that." He pointed to the dirty streaks across her driver door and then touched a spot on her cheek. She reached up and felt grease. Of course. Her shirt was already ruined, so she gladly used the sleeve to wipe it away.

"Time for someone else to watch these monsters besides you." Like a panther stalking his prey, Eric waited for the boys to run past again, and then he reached out and scooped up both of them, one under each arm. They squealed like little piglets, laughing and protesting, but he held them firm.

Anne grabbed the rags out of their hands and dropped them in a nearby garbage can. When Eric brought the boys over to the spigot where she'd filled the bucket, she turned it on and scrubbed their squirmy faces, hands, and feet while Eric held them in place. Then Eric squelched his way through the mud and set them down on the bottom step of the porch. The boys took off into the house the second he let them go.

She figured Eric would take off his boots and follow, but instead, he turned and made his way back to where she was crouching next to the spigot. The ground around her on all sides was now an oozing, muddy mess.

"Come on, let's get you out of there." He said it like she was a skittish colt, and that's exactly how she felt with his arms outstretched toward her.

"It's not quicksand. I'm fine." She stood and strode toward him right through the mud, determined not to need Eric's rescue again on this trip, and all was fine until her shoe slid sideways and she quickly realized she was about to do the splits against her will.

"Anne," he growled, lunging toward her. He caught her, but only enough to break her fall as they both slid down into the mud bog, sitting side-by-side in ooze.

The feel of cold mud seeping through the seat of her jeans was just about the worst sensation ever.

It was a laugh or cry moment, and Anne put the back of her hand against her mouth to keep from doing either.

Eric stared at her for several seconds before reaching up and wiping one muddy finger down her nose. He smiled, daring her to back down from the gauntlet he'd just thrown.

Against her better judgement, she decided to take him up on it. Smiling back, she pressed her hand into the mud and then wrapped that same hand around the back of his neck. He didn't even flinch.

He stared at her a long time before picking up more mud and pressing it against the hollow of her neck, his fingers trailing there probably longer than was appropriate.

Anne shivered, with cold, and with something else she didn't dare name. This was still a mud fight. Nothing more.

She pressed some mud into his hair, letting her fingers massage it in.

He drew a line of mud across her forehead.

Someone cleared their throat above them, and Anne looked up, letting her hand drop from Eric's hair.

Benneck tilted his head, studying them. "I'm sorry. Am I interrupting some strange mating ritual?"

"Not at all." Eric got to his feet before extending a hand out to help Anne up. She stayed on her feet out of sheer will.

Benneck shook his head, looking at the two of them. "A lot of help you two are. I just wanted to let you know the car's ready for a test run, and um, a car wash. Not that you two mud monsters are in any shape to get inside a car."

***

Eric wasn't sure he could explain his momentary loss of all common sense even if he wanted to. And boy, he really didn't want to. He stripped down in the doorway of his cabin and ran in his boxers to the bathroom. Sophie and Adam were off on a day trip and they'd taken Trapper with them, so not even the dog was there to judge his life choices.

Not wanting to clog the shower drain with excess dirt, Eric pulled handfuls of mud out of his hair and dropped it in the little trashcan in the corner.

His reflection in the mirror betrayed how conflicted he felt. His eyes were a little too bright, and his mouth twitched, at moments threatening to break into a smile before he went back to frowning at his own stupidity. Yes, he had kept things friendly with Lucy today, not making a move when it was obvious she wanted him to kiss her. But that didn't mean he wasn't dancing on a thin line while he waffled with indecision.

He had to get away from Anne. That was all there was to it. He'd spent too many years carefully avoiding ever seeing her again to ruin it all now.

After his shower, he hurried and dressed before jogging back out to Benneck, who was sitting in the driver's seat of Anne's car. Anne was nowhere in sight.

Benneck motioned for him to get in, which he did.

"How bad is it?" Eric asked.

"I'm not sure yet, and I'd prefer we drive this around ourselves, just so I can freely talk about what a piece of junk it is. I only fixed a few things. Her best bet is to sell it to a Mercedes fanatic who can restore it to its former glory. She hasn't done any maintenance on this thing at all beyond oil changes."

Benneck started it up, and they sat listening to it idle, waiting for the rattling to start.

"So far so good." Benneck put it in drive and they slowly made their way out to the main road. After a few more minutes with no apparent issues, Benneck turned to look at Eric. "So, not that it's any of my business, but what exactly happened back there?"

"She slipped in the mud."

"Uh-huh. And it just naturally followed the two of you

should finger paint each other?"

"You make it sound dirty." Eric realized he'd made a terrible pun about the same time Benneck did, and they both laughed.

"Benneck, are you interested in Anne?" They were good enough friends that Eric knew he could outright ask, and Benneck would give him an honest answer.

"It's never going to happen for me again. You know that. Don't worry, you are free and clear to pursue her."

Eric shook his head. "That's not why I asked."

"And what about Lucy?" Benneck countered.

"I don't know yet. But there's nothing between Anne and me. Not that it matters. We're going to San Fran and she's off to do her father's bidding in Malibu."

"No, she's not." Benneck gave him a puzzled look. "Actually, she'll be doing Mary's bidding. In San Francisco."

"Who told you that?" Eric asked as alarm began to build up inside of him. He and Lucy already had a date planned to go see a movie at the iconic Foreign Cinema. Lucy had all sorts of ideas about showing him her favorite San Francisco haunts. It was his chance to start over, without seeing Anne again.

"Anne told me. She'll be helping out Mary's nanny when she's not working at the natural history museum."

"You're sure?"

"Why don't you double-check with Anne?" Benneck raised an eyebrow. "Or is there a particular reason the two of you only allow long looks from afar and occasional mud baths together as your only form of communication?"

"You're never going to let that go, are you?"

"Never."

Eric sighed. "Okay, here's the thing about Anne and me..."

CHAPTER 7 ♥ ENJOY THE CIRCUS THAT IS HER FAMILY

Mary stormed into Anne's bedroom, her chest puffing in and out in an air of deep offense.
Anne stopped organizing her suitcase and sat down on the bed next to it. Whatever this was wouldn't be resolved until Mary had her say. "What's the matter?"
"Daddy is insisting we meet him in L.A. on our way back to San Francisco. He somehow thinks I have room for all the furniture he couldn't sell after they moved out of the mansion. It's in some storage unit in a terrible part of town. Like I want to rent a moving truck and hire movers to haul it all out of there. It's all ancient, impossibly heavy, and gaudy anyway." Mary shook her cellphone at Anne. "I suggested he donate the things, and you should have heard him squawk. You'd think the Queen of Sheba herself carved his bureau drawers. He's impossible."
He was impossible; that wasn't an exaggeration. Mary on one of her tirades actually mimicked Dad quite well, but that wasn't something Anne would ever point out. To either of them.
"What does he want you to do with all of it?" Anne asked.
"Keep it! Heaven knows you don't need it, being single and all. And he said Lizzie already took the things she wants and used them to decorate the new condo."

Anne ignored the assumption she wouldn't want anything. She was used to it by now. And it wasn't worth the fight even if she did want something. Instead, her mind dwelled on the fees from a storage unit adding up. Sketchy part of town or not, Dad would have rented out the largest unit at an exorbitant rate. There was no such thing as cheap storage in California.

"It is on the way. We can at least go look."

Mary sighed. "On the way or not, he'll want to chat, and somehow my boys will have to sit perfectly still or it will annoy him. I'd rather stand my ground and tell him no over the phone. He already shipped all your bedroom furniture to my place. What else could we want? That gigantic harp he used to keep in the music room?" Mary giggled. "Or the bust of Beethoven he kept on a pedestal next to it?"

"Those both sold," Anne admitted.

Mary tapped her fingers against the wall, lost in thought. "You could go meet him. And that way if your car starts to act up, you can get one of those car trailers and pull it behind a moving van."

"I thought you didn't want anything."

"You could take pictures and send them to me. And I'd tell you yes or no."

There was a calculating look in Mary's eye she tried to hide under a casual, thoughtful gaze. Had she thrown a fit just to reach this exact conclusion? The ways of Mary were a mystery too murky to unravel.

Anne stood and went back to packing. "Give me some time to think about it." And think she did, along with several Google searches on her phone. A U-Haul tow dolly was an inexpensive option she hadn't considered. She could pay for it, while Mary and Carl could pay for the moving truck. That way, she didn't have to put more miles on a car that could act up again at any moment. Benneck didn't give her a lot of hope as to the car's longevity without a lot more work on it.

"Anne! Dinner!"

Anne got up and left the room. It was her last night here, and she and Eric had been doing an exemplary job of avoiding each other after the mud incident. Lucy monopolized his attention now that Etta and Hayden spent most of their time in the hot tub on the back porch.

It would be even easier to avoid each other once the vacation was over. San Francisco was a big city, and Anne planned to keep herself too busy to even think about the man.

***

Having spent years of his life sitting in a cockpit, one would think Eric wouldn't mind a seven-hour car trip, but it seemed like this vacation would never end. He was itching to get back to a regular work schedule and a to-do list long enough to keep his mind off Anne. The barely-moving traffic on the interstate only reminded him of why he loved to fly so much.

He looked over at Lucy and smiled. She was awfully sleepy for a co-pilot. They didn't even make it to San Bernardino before she passed out, resting her head on her jacket wedged against the window. For all the scheming she'd done in order to catch a ride with him back to San Francisco, she sure wasn't taking advantage of the situation well. All the better. He had no intention of turning their friendship into a full-blown relationship anytime soon.

He inched his truck forward, relieved when he saw that the lane previously blocked by traffic cones was opening up just ahead. A special gift from the road construction fairies.

Etta and Hayden had decided to take the route up through Victorville so they could stop off at the Route 66 Museum. Perhaps they had been wiser. Going through L.A. was only faster if you could drive at speed.

His phone rang, and he picked it up from the cup holder. "Hey, Benneck. I'm hoping you left early enough to miss this pileup. I'm finally starting to move again and get through L.A."

"Perfect timing. I'm here in Highland Park with Anne and we need you."

"Car trouble?"

"Not exactly. Mary talked her into picking up a bunch of furniture from her dad's storage unit, renting a moving truck, and loading it all by herself."

Eric groaned. "Of course she did."

"I weaseled the story out of her when I called to see how she was doing. Anne told me not to come help, which of course meant I was totally going to come. But I'm not the knight-in-shining-armor she's hoping for, no matter what she says. This is your chance."

Eric rested his head back. "My chance to what? Strain my back?"

"To make things right. Seize this second chance with her. Or just enjoy the circus that is her family. Her father and sister just got here, and they brought the ugly cat!"

"Beauregard?"

"So you *were* listening to us the other night. Are you coming to help or not?"

"Not." Eric glanced over at Lucy, assured she was still asleep. She'd be mortified if she knew she slept with her mouth wide open like that. He owed it to her to keep his focus on his destination, which did not include rescuing Anne once again. Not that Anne ever asked to be rescued. She just seemed to find trouble in her attempts to help everyone else.

Besides... seeing her family again? The last time he'd been in the same room with her father, the man had told him over his dead body was Anne getting married at twenty and divorced at twenty-one. That Eric was immature and a bad influence on her. And Anne had listened. She'd let Eric walk out and hadn't followed him. Enough thinking about Anne. He gripped the steering wheel and focused on the road.

"Eric, in all seriousness, I could use someone who can actually lift furniture here."

"It can't be me. I'm sorry."

"I think you're making a serious mistake. I know how you feel about her, and she's not lost to you forever. My Jenny is never coming back. The only thing keeping you and Anne apart is your stubborn pride."

Eric blinked in shock. He didn't know what to say to that. Benneck never talked about Jenny. He talked around her death with his occasional gloomy comments, but he hadn't mentioned her by name in months. What had Anne done to him, and why was he so set on this matchmaking?

"Benneck, did you listen to me at all? Her family took one look at me, and suddenly our engagement became this bad idea we were rushing into. She chose them over me. Nothing has changed. The second one of them needs something, Anne is there, no matter what the cost. I can't be sucked back into that." He glanced over at Lucy again, praying she wouldn't wake up in the middle of this conversation.

Benneck sighed. "Okay, I didn't want to have to say this, but there's a guy here her family brought along. He's starring in a movie with Anne's dad, and he seems to have no problem volunteering to help. And the way he looks at Anne... I'm just saying, Anne's the real deal. You're not the only one who's going to see that in her. So make your move now, or don't. I'll shut up now."

Eric felt his irritation rising, but he wouldn't chew out Benneck for being a hopeless romantic. It was just the way the man was wired. He didn't understand. Nobody understood the utter devastation and betrayal Eric felt when Anne gave him back her engagement ring. It had colored everything else in his life after it. And if he tried to let it go only to get hurt again... He couldn't do that. Anne hadn't wanted him then, and there was nothing to suggest she wanted him back now.

"I have to get Lucy home. Good luck with the move." Eric hung up and set his phone face-down on the console.

***

Anne had heard much about Hollywood heartthrob Wyatt Ellis starting back when he attended the same exclusive prep school as her sister and ran in the same popular circles. Lizzie had been sure he would ask her to prom her junior year, but alas, he went with someone else. But today was the first time Anne had ever actually seen the man in person.

He was the golden boy personified: glowing tan, light curls, toned body, and a smile that could light up a Crest toothpaste commercial. If he and Lizzie were chummy now, he was doing a very good job of hiding it. He had positioned himself next to Anne, and his attention only turned to Lizzie when she talked baby talk to her cat in his little purse carrier, as she was doing now, shaking her blonde bangs in the cat's face.

"Beauregard, my little darling, we'll be home soon, and I'll make you a special lunch. You'll love it. Won't you? Won't you?" She held up his little paw before kissing it. The cat stared back at her with a look of long-suffering indifference.

Wyatt smothered a laugh. "That cat looks like the inside of a mummy. Does Lizzie sleep with it? Its eyes would terrify me at night."

"He has a little bed next to hers," Anne admitted. It was a baby bassinet with a white gauzy canopy over it, but she decided not to mention that part.

Penelope, the friend Lizzie had brought along, tried to pet Beauregard and was rewarded with a hiss.

"He's just hangry," Lizzie assured her. "I know deep down he loves his Penelope. Doesn't he? Doesn't he?"

Lizzie was convinced everyone loved Penelope. Secretly, Anne thought the cat had the right idea. She felt like hissing too whenever Penelope was around. The woman was like a skin rash, everywhere and almost impossible to get rid of. Her ringing laugh, the echo chamber of every inane thing Lizzie said, had always grated on Anne's nerves.

Anne closed her eyes for a second and prayed for forgiveness. It had to be a sin to dislike someone so much. Unfortunately, Penelope had that rare quality of living up to every bad assumption Anne had ever made about her. She was a bad influence on Lizzie. Worse, Anne feared Penelope had set her sights on Dad, hoping to become wife number three.

Why else would he suddenly start dressing like a millennial going through a bad-boy phase? Today, he was wearing a leather jacket and distressed skinny jeans with a chain attaching his wallet to his belt loop. He'd let his stubble grow out, but dyed it an even brown color, and his hair was buzzed all the way up the sides, but long and wavy on top.

Anne watched as Penelope tugged on the arm of his jacket and whispered something in his ear, making him smile. No, this couldn't be happening.

"Do you think if you stare at her long enough lasers will shoot out of your eyes?" Wyatt murmured in her ear.

Anne ducked her head. "Maybe. It worked for Matilda."

"Who?"

"She's a little girl in a Roald Dahl book. Never mind." No one ever got her book references. Anne went back to typing out a list of items for Mary, not that Mary had responded to any of her texts so far. This move hadn't even started, and it was already a disaster.

Wyatt dropped his head close to hers so he could see her list. "Just put gold-plated everything, and I think that will cover it."

"So true." Anne stared at the stack of gilded mirrors in every shape and size wrapped carefully in bubble wrap and stacked against the wall of the storage unit. It was an excessive collection, and it didn't even include the larger mirrors that had sold.

Wyatt stole her phone and typed out something quickly before she could grab it back. If she didn't know better, she'd think he was flirting with her.

She looked at her phone. ***Dad's changing the will.*** He'd sent it to Mary.

"What did you do that for?"

"It seemed like something that would make her stop ignoring you. Will it?"

"She's probably stuck in a mountain pass and isn't getting any of these messages. But yes, she'll respond to that. Not for any need for money. She just wouldn't want to be left out of the loop."

"I rest my case." Wyatt crossed his arms, looking satisfied with himself.

"Do I get to send out messages on your phone now?" Anne asked, holding out her hand palm up. Celebrities always assumed any liberty they took was okay because of who they were. But she doubted he would like her swiping his phone and sending eye-catching messages to his contacts.

"Another time, dear Anne. Another time."

Exactly. She looked over at Benneck, who had just finished up a furtive phone call. She hoped her suspicions weren't correct and it wasn't Eric he'd been talking to. She'd made Benneck promise he wouldn't, which was exactly why she was so worried he would.

"So," Wyatt said, rubbing his hands together. "As much as I enjoy reenacting a scene from Storage Wars, let's get done whatever it is we're doing here. I have a meeting at one." He checked his watch. "I say we give Mary one more minute, and then you decide what goes and what stays."

"Agreed." Anne wondered what hold her father had over Wyatt that he would even come along. Yes, he was filming a movie with Dad, but there had to be some other connection she wasn't seeing. Maybe they were gambling on set and this was Wyatt's way of paying off a debt.

She waved Benneck over. "Let's take it all." If she ended up dropping the lot of it off at a thrift store on her way home, so be it. Her father could pay the last month's rent on the storage unit and be done with it.

Benneck and Wyatt got to work, moving furniture up the truck ramp and stacking it carefully. If Wyatt's agent knew he was lifting heavy objects and walking backwards up a truck ramp, he'd likely have a fit. But she wasn't about to point that out.

"Anne." Her father came over and put his arm around her. She dropped her head on his shoulder just for a moment. The leather of his jacket was cold, but gave off his familiar scent of clove gum and Christian Dior cologne. He gave her a light squeeze. "Thank you for bringing all this to Mary for me. What would we ever do without you?"

Anne sighed. "Oh, you'd do just fine."

"Baah. You're a comfort to me, you know that, right?" He turned to scrutinize her face, and she braced herself for whatever was coming next. She would choose to focus on the kind words already given, no matter what else he said.

"Are you wearing a moisturizer with a strong enough sunscreen? Your skin looks very dry and weathered."

"Yes, I'm using moisturizer, but I did just come back from camping."

"Well, wear more. Your neck looks dry too. Make sure to use it on your neck and shoulders. People forget their necks age and are as visible as the rest of their skin."

"I'll do that."

He went back to overseeing the move, calling out for them to be careful with the wine cabinet, and Anne felt fortunate to get off with only a lecture on skincare.

She'd learned long ago not to mind what her father said about her looks. It wasn't worth attempting the perfection he would never see in her. Besides, a person was so much more than how they looked at any given moment. Which was such an ironic thought as she admired Benneck and Wyatt working together, their muscles rippling as they lifted furniture. They were both extremely attractive men, and yet she felt no zing for either of them. Thoughts of Eric seeped in, and she bit her thumbnail, irritated that she couldn't stop wishing for things she would never have.

She jogged into the storage unit and pushed the last of the items from the back to the front, making sure nothing got left behind. Work was the only effective antidote for brooding.

Benneck gripped her in a hug when he was done, now panting and sweaty, and only laughed when she wrinkled her nose. "All right, Anne. I'm calling in all my favors when we get to San Francisco. Cookies, personal tours. Your firstborn has to be named after me. Even if it's a girl."

Anne sighed. "I thought for a moment you were going to ask for my firstborn, Rumpelstiltskin."

"We're almost to that point, Anne. Almost. Now that the truck is packed, we need to drive it back to the rental place and hook the car trailer to it. I'll meet you over there, okay?"

"Okay." She kissed his cheek.

She blushed when she saw Wyatt watching the exchange with more curiosity than she felt comfortable acknowledging. He approached her after Benneck left in his car, his eyes never leaving hers.

Putting both hands on her shoulders, he gave her what could only be described as a self-conscious smolder. As if he was trying to appear both confident and vulnerable. Would she always think of Wyatt in terms of his acting?

"Anne, after this movie wraps up, I'd like to lay low for a while before the promotion hounds descend. I have a beachfront house in San Francisco, and I'd love to come see you. Dinner sometime? How does that sound?"

Confusing. It sounded confusing. She shouldn't be suspicious. It was just dinner, and it wasn't that she believed herself to be unattractive. But Wyatt Ellis? He dated supermodels. He must want to be friends, and she'd need friends as much as he seemed to.

"Yes, of course. That would be nice."

"Brilliant." Wyatt broke into a smile that could revive a dying world. It was award-winning really. Almost too perfect to trust.

CHAPTER 8 ♥ HE WALKED INTO A TRAP OF HIS OWN MAKING

Eric had never arrived for work in such a high-stress, high-excitement atmosphere. For Adam, who was retired, this was a fun new hobby. But for Benneck and Eric, this was a risky career change with a brand-new company. They were both leaving behind a steady job at an airline where they had seniority, a dependable benefits package, and a 401K.

Eric tried to focus on the positive. He was trading all that for something better. There would be no more bidding on routes, being gone for weeks at a time, or living out of a hotel. No sleeping in an unfamiliar bed during the day so he had the required rest hours to pilot a red-eye flight to another part of the world.

The charter business their wealthy friend, Curt Harville, had created focused on short flights in and out of San Francisco for business people and wealthy families who traveled regularly. The schedule was about as predictable as you could get for a venture like this.

Today, Eric and Benneck would fly a CEO and his family to their private cabin in Washington State, take six passengers from Seattle to L.A., and then a group of five passengers from L.A.

back to San Francisco. They'd be done, paperwork and all, by six p.m.

The business's profitability hinged on its proprietary scheduling software, which allowed them to create flight plans in the most efficient and cost-effective ways. In the foggy summer, they also had a location advantage, being out of the Bay. While the main airport suffered constant delays, they would be able to leave on time, and they were constantly looking for other ways to get an edge over the competition.

Eric jogged out to help Benneck with the preflight check. They didn't speak while moving down the checklist, examining the flaps and ailerons, the propellers, and the fuel tanks. But once they were done, Benneck nodded toward the steps leading up into the plane.

"Have you met Connie yet?" Benneck asked.

"Yep." He knew what Benneck was getting at without him having to say it. Connie, the flight attendant, had an intense stare not softened by her frequent wide smiles, but she was dedicated to her job, and that was all that mattered. Not everyone could cater to the rich and entitled's every whim with polite precision in such a small space. It was certainly something Eric had to consider when he quit his job, got type rated for these smaller chartered jets, and became a private commercial pilot. Every seat was a step above first class, and the customers expected to be treated as such.

Here they came now. The family they'd be flying walked out of the lounge, while an attendant wheeled out their matching Gucci luggage.

Connie poked her head out of the plane's door, then jogged down the steps to greet them, pulling open a sun umbrella to hold over the woman's head as they walked and talked. Connie began nodding vigorously, already taking orders from her.

"Here we go," said Benneck.

They followed the family into the plane and introduced themselves. Everything inside was white leather with accents of gold. Eric fully expected the kids to get up on the plush furniture or knock things over, but they were sweet and well-behaved, obviously used to traveling like this. They showed no curiosity whatsoever, not even about the cockpit, which had no door separating it from the rest of the plane.

After a weather check and a go-ahead from the tower for takeoff, Eric lifted them into the sky, marveling at how seamless it all was without a security line, hundreds of passengers to seat, or fights over overhead baggage bins.

Benneck looked over at him once they reached climbing altitude. "Do you have plans tonight? You know you can have those now."

"Why, do you have plans?" asked Eric.

"I asked first."

"You know, you've gotten really annoying since you met Anne."

"Who said this was about Anne?" Benneck grinned, clearly happy he got Eric to mention her first.

"I do have plans tonight, actually. Hold on, Bellingham is radioing."

They listened to the airport's updates on landing in Washington before Benneck reminded him he hadn't revealed his after-work plans yet.

"Lucy and I are going to grab dinner at this seafood place she knows about. I told her I'd text her when I had a better idea of how late I'll be."

Benneck grunted. Eric knew Benneck didn't like Lucy, or rather, didn't like the idea of Eric dating Lucy.

"Great. Anne and I will join you. I love seafood."

"You're not invited," Eric said, knowing he didn't mean it. The fact that Benneck wanted to have plans at all was a huge step forward. Prior to agreeing to come on Eric's camping trip, there was little that would get Benneck to leave his apartment unless it was work related. The war inside Eric started up a new battle. He'd forever be indebted to Anne for helping Benneck return to the land of the living, and yet he also wished it had been someone else.

Seeing Anne again had opened up a wound he didn't want to feel anymore. He missed her all over again. He missed her smile, her voice, her observant, quiet way of taking in the world. And if Benneck had his way, which was most of the time, Eric wouldn't only be reminded of Anne, he would be hanging out with her. Somehow, he had to make this work. He turned his thoughts to Lucy. She really was a great person, fun to be around. Tonight would be fine. The four of them could hang out as friends, just like at the cabin.

***

Anne marched her last tour group past the recreations of a Neolithic village and on towards the dinosaur climber. It was time for the kids to get some wiggles out before they were packed like sardines onto their bus for the ride back to their summer camp. Anne thought about Colter and Charlie and what sort of mischief they might have caused to be uninvited back to theirs. She could imagine several possibilities, knowing them.

Even in the summer, the museum had school and city rec groups constantly coming and going, enough that they would pass each other in the halls, and Anne would watch carefully to make sure no one got mixed up.

She liked leading tours and was good at it. There was a certain rush that came from stepping out of her comfort zone and demanding a group's attention. It was a little like being an informative stand-up comedian.

"Step, step, one, two, three," Anne sang out. "Who's the fiercest dinosaur? Triceratops or Stegosaurus?"

The kids hollered back their opinion, which, as always, was to abandon both options she gave in favor of the T-Rex.

Anne shook her head, pretending to be offended on behalf of the Triceratops and Stegosaurus. "The Tyrannosaurus Rex doesn't even have any spikes. Boo!"

The kids laughed and hurried to catch up to her. Their teacher threw Anne a grateful look, as she'd been wrangling kids off the velvet rope divider pretty much the entire time.

The museum wasn't as kid-friendly as it could be, but Anne wasn't in any position to suggest changes. Right now, her job was to prove herself and carve out a place here. She had one ally, a friend from high school who was more down on her luck than Anne. With her chronic pain, Beth only worked occasionally, and it was clear their boss hoped she'd quit for good.

The other tour guides were mostly retired volunteers and fell into two camps—overly-friendly and welcoming, or prickly and suspicious of change, especially staff changes. Anne would steer clear of that second group until she could win them over.

Having reached their last stop, Anne waved the kids forward. "Come meet Izzy the Isisaurus. She's guarding her nest of eggs."

Anne and their teacher helped them line up so they could go down the dinosaur slide and check out Izzy's nest at the bottom.

After this group left and she had cleaned up after them, her shift at the museum would end, and another one would begin when she got home: taking Charlie and Colter into the backyard and out of Mary's hair. Life would be busy and harried, and that was exactly what Anne needed these days.

"Is that the real size of an Isisaurus?" a little boy asked, tugging on her sleeve. "In the dinosaur book I have it says they don't really know how big they were."

Anne bent down to his level. "It's true. Scientists haven't found a full skeleton of this one, so they did some guesswork about the length of its tail and its full height. Now, if this were my exhibit, I'd add a snake lying hidden nearby the nest. They think there was one that preyed on dinosaur nests like this one in India, waiting for the eggs to hatch. The snake was called a Sanajeh."

The boy's eyes grew wide, and Anne worried for a moment that she had scared him, but then he broke out in a huge grin and ran off to tell everyone else about the prehistoric baby-eating snake. Soon several kids were pretending to be snakes and a scream fest ignited. Anne smiled. A little chaos was a good thing in the pursuit of knowledge.

The teacher whistled for the kids' attention, and they all

gathered around her while she did a head count. Anne walked the group out the back doors to the bus line and waved goodbye once they had all left, leaving a cloud of exhaust behind them. Then she went back inside to get her purse and lunch bag out of her locker. She had three missed texts.

One was from Mary making sure she was coming to get the boys before they tore the house apart. She quickly responded that she was on her way now.

Another was from Benneck reminding her they were going out tonight. She wasn't sure if he was being intentionally vague or if, like her, he just didn't care what they did as long as they did something. She would respond to Benneck's text right after she solved the mystery of the last text.

It was from a number she didn't recognize, and the words, *hey, it's me*, didn't help either. For one heart-stopping moment she considered whether it was from Eric. There hadn't been a re-exchange of phone numbers between them, and why would there be? Besides, it would be easy for him to get her number from Benneck if he wanted it.

She sat down on the bench in the employee lounge and stared at those three little words. Best to not make assumptions until she knew for sure.

Hey, me. Is this meant to be a guessing game?

When she didn't get a response right away, she gathered up her things and walked out. The little ping coming from her back pocket had her pulling her phone out again to check.

If you'd like.
Is this my future self checking in?
Nope. Try again.
Are you family?
Wrong again.
Are you male?
Last I checked.

Anne smiled. Who was this guy? Eric would not be this playful with her. Not now. Maybe it was some random person who liked to message strange numbers for fun. It was time to get to the bottom of this.

I'm heading out to my car so I'll say farewell for now unless you'd like to identify yourself.

The response came quickly. *I'm an especially handsome mover. And don't ask if this is Benneck because I'm way better looking than he is.*

The, *hey it's me*, made a lot more sense now. Only someone a bit self-absorbed would assume a person he met once would know him right off. And Wyatt Ellis, while nice enough, was a bit self-absorbed. How could he not be when everyone around him told him how wonderful he was?

Hi, Wyatt.

She sent the text off before getting in her car and putting her phone away despite the continued dings of new messages. It was a short commute, but San Francisco traffic was a beast best managed with one's full attention. Not to mention, it would do the guy some good to have to wait a few minutes for a response.

She yawned when she pulled into the long driveway and spotted Charlie and Colter waiting for her on the front step. Just looking at their pent-up energy made her tired.

She got out of the car and held her arms open when they ran over to greet her.

Charlie gave her a big hug, resting his pointy chin against her stomach as he stared up at her. "Mom said if she sees me use my shirt as a napkin one more time she'll scream. But she screamed already."

Colter laughed. "She screamed 'cause you took that bug out of your pocket and showed it to her."

"It died," Charlie said with a knowing nod, as if Mary would have been fine with a live bug, but a dead one coming out of his pocket was too much.

"Can we play detectives now?" Colter tugged on her hand, pulling her along as he explained the game, which involved Anne coming across the boys in the yard playing dead, and then trying to decide who had murdered them. Apparently, their nanny nixed the idea, but it was too good for them not to try again with someone else. They figured Anne might be game. And she was. After all, she wasn't worried about being fired or corrupting their minds. The joys of being an aunt.

They played until the sun went down, with the stories and clues getting sillier and sillier. They had finally convinced Anne it was her turn to play dead, and after they hid around the corner, she obediently sprawled in the grass with her eyes closed, clutching a half-eaten Snickers bar from her purse. To make the scene more convincing, she'd wiped a little bit of chocolate onto her upper lip. She focused on keeping a straight face when she heard the sound of little feet and giggling coming closer.

The back of Anne's neck tickled from the grass and she turned her head slightly, just to relieve the itch before holding still once again. Playing dead was a serious art.

"Look, it's a body."

"Oh, no. It's Annie."

"She was poisoned! Who did this to our Annie? We'll make them suffer."

"Oh, yeah. Suffer hard."

She could hear them circling her, and then both boys shrieked. One of them shouted, "Don't touch the candy bar. It's deadly."

"I'll take my chances," said a familiar masculine voice as the Snickers was swiped from her hand. Anne opened her eyes and sat up quickly, only to see Benneck and Eric kneeling in the grass, watching her with amused faces. Benneck ate the last bite of her chocolate before crumpling up the wrapper and sticking it in his pocket.

"You ready to go have some fun, Anne?" Benneck asked.

"She's having fun with us," Colter whined.

Anne reached out and took Colter's sweaty, little hand. "It's getting too dark to play out here. Aren't you ready to go inside for dinner?" She pulled out her phone, alarmed to see it was almost seven o-clock.

"Yeah, go get dinner before I beat you to it and eat it all." Benneck raced the two boys across the grass and up the decks stairs, letting them pass him up at the last minute. They reached the sliding door and slammed it in his face, laughing in triumph. Anne watched with a smile before turning back to meet Eric's gaze. Would she ever run out of embarrassing predicaments for him to find her in?

It wasn't until Eric pointed to his own lip that she remembered the chocolate. She swiped at her lips with the back of her hand, feeling like an idiot.

"Is it still there?" she asked, willing her face not to turn red. There was no helping her hair, coming loose from its ponytail and likely filled with random bits of grass.

Eric reached out his thumb and wiped at the corner of her mouth, setting the butterflies in her stomach into flight. "Now it's all gone."

"Thanks," she ducked her head, wishing she felt less, that his touch meant nothing to her.

It was a relief when Benneck returned, and she was ready with an excuse not to go anywhere tonight. Being tired was not a lie. She was tired. And in desperate need of a shower. The two guys could go have fun without her.

She plucked out a blade of grass and twisted it between her fingers. "Benneck, I'm tired. I think I'll stay here and watch a movie. You're welcome to join me or go out with Eric. I won't mind."

Eric ran a hand through his hair. "Actually, Lucy and I are going to a seaside restaurant."

"And we're coming with them," Benneck said, holding out a hand to help her up.

Anne glared at him, but she accepted the boost to her feet. It would have been nice to know about the dinner date plans earlier. "You don't need me there. Go have fun with Lucy and Eric."

"And be their third wheel? No way. Help me out here, Eric."

***

Of course. Because what they really needed was to involve Eric in their argument, and for Eric to encourage Anne to spend time with him when she clearly didn't want to. No matter what he said, it would be the wrong thing.

If there was anything he knew about Anne, it was that being tired was a flimsy cover for what was actually bothering her. She didn't want to be around him but would never say it.

He shouldn't want to be around her either, even if she was the most maddening, adorable, surprising woman he'd ever known. There were layers to her now that hadn't been there when they were both young college students. Her willingness to engage in mischief with her nephews, for one. If she was this carefree as an aunt, what must she be like as a tour guide? As a friend? As more?

He needed to make a clean break before he lost his head, and unfortunately, that meant not hanging out with Lucy anymore either. After tonight, he'd untangle himself from that situation too. He regretted ever thinking Lucy was a good candidate for attempting dating again, even just as friends. He would need someone not connected to Anne. Someone who couldn't even remind him of her.

"I think Anne can make up her own mind." He hadn't meant it to sound like a dig at their past, but when her eyes narrowed slightly, he knew that's how she took it. So much for trying to remain neutral.

She turned back to Benneck. "I'll make everyone late. I'm not exactly ready to go anywhere."

"The restaurant is only a few blocks away, and we didn't plan to go until eight. Lucy's meeting us here. Go get ready, and if we need to leave before then, I'll send Eric and Lucy along without us. I promise."

Anne smiled. "That's not exactly encouragement to hurry." She meant it as a gentle tease, but Benneck didn't smile back.

"This conversation is making me tired." He dropped his head, looking defeated. "I give up. Never mind, I'll just head home and you can call me when you feel like making plans." He started walking off, the little manipulator. Sometimes Benneck's quick mood changes made Eric so mad, especially when he used them to get people to drop their side of an argument.

Eric was about to say something when Anne jogged around Benneck and stuck her finger in his chest. "Don't do that. Don't try to trap me with guilt when I just found out about these plans. I'll get ready as fast as I can. But that means you don't make Eric and Lucy wait on me. Okay?"

"Okay." Benneck waved her towards the house, and she took off running, her loose ponytail bouncing behind her. Benneck slowly walked back to Eric, now looking even more morose. His charm hadn't worked on Anne the way he thought it would. It had to be a bruise to the ego.

Eric couldn't help feeling a shot of admiration for Anne, and then regret for allowing himself to notice. He was proud of her; that was all. It didn't have to mean anything.

With the last of their sunlight quickly disappearing, Eric and Benneck came up to the deck to sit and wait. Mary and Carl's deck was a HGTV show-off piece. The beautiful redwood gleamed under the lights at the tops of all the railings, and the matching deck furniture was surprisingly comfortable. Through the sliding glass window they could see the large screen TV blaring a cartoon as the boys sat in front of it and ate their dinners. Mary was nowhere in sight.

Lucy arrived right at seven-thirty, and Benneck gave up the deck chair next to Eric and went to lean against the railing, looking out over the yard. She was happy to wait for Anne, and promised not to say a word about it. Benneck really was like a little puppet-master, making things happen the way he wanted them to.

Lucy, bubbly as always, asked about their day. Her hand came to rest on Eric's forearm as he talked. Her slim fingers were warm against his skin. The show of affection was a natural progression in their relationship, at least from her point-of-view. And yet, Eric's insides froze at her touch. He wished he could fast forward through this night already, to where he put his plan in motion to undo it all. To never see Lucy again. To never see

Anne again. To start over. Again.

It had to be done for his own sanity. He had walked into a trap of his own making because he couldn't make up his mind. His heart wasn't ready to let Anne go. There was no use in continuing to deny it. He still loved her.

The truth of it hit him in full force when Anne walked out a half-hour later, her hair down and sleek, makeup done, wearing a sundress that hit just above the knee, showing off her smooth legs.

He forced his eyes away, only to catch Benneck watching him, knowing exactly what Eric had been thinking. It was the first time Benneck had smiled since Anne's scolding.

Eric punched him in the shoulder when they turned to follow the girls down the stairs. "Save it."

Benneck held his hands up in surrender. "I'm not saying a word."

They drove in Eric's car, Lucy sitting shotgun next to him, and Anne and Benneck in back. Lucy filled in the gaps in conversation, telling them about the restaurant and the beachfront below it where people often played sand volleyball until late.

The city buzzed with an energy only matched by Lucy's enthusiasm. Her eyes often turned to see Eric's reaction to it all. He smiled, not pulling away when she took his free hand, though his instincts cried out to let go. He could be a good date for one night. It certainly wasn't Lucy's fault he was a mess inside.

Every time Eric looked at the back seat, Benneck and Anne had their heads together, laughing about something on her phone. Eric focused his attention back on following Lucy's directions for where the best place was to park.

After they reached the restaurant doors and put their names in with the hostess, they found a bench outside and squished in together. Lucy claimed to be cold and snuggled into Eric's side. He didn't mean to listen in on Benneck and Anne's whispered conversation, but with Lucy quiet for the moment, it carried over to his ears.

"Guys don't text for no reason," Benneck murmured. "These are more than friendly check-ins."

"So, what's his reason?"

"You tell me. He said he's coming to see you, right?"

"He says."

"Anne. Be careful with this guy."

"I'm always careful. That's the last thing you should worry about with me."

"Well, be careful anyway."

Lucy picked her head up from Eric's shoulder and looked over at the pair. "Who should Anne be careful with?"

Anne frowned at her phone. "No one."

"Wyatt Ellis is not exactly no one," Benneck said, flinching before Anne even elbowed him.

"Wyatt Ellis!" Lucy's jaw dropped. "No way. You know him, Anne?"

"Sort of." Anne waved off Lucy's excitement. "He knows my father is all."

"How lucky to hobnob with celebrities all the time. I can't imagine." Lucy's smile turned sly. "So, how does Benneck feel about having competition for your affection?"

Benneck looked straight at Eric. "I'm fine with it. Bring it on."

Eric glared right back before pulling his phone out and Googling Wyatt Ellis. He recognized the name, but wasn't sure he was thinking of the right celebrity. Dang, the search results immediately proved him wrong. Wyatt Ellis was better looking and more famous that the guy Eric had been thinking of. He had also dated his way through most of Hollywood, though his last public relationship had ended almost a year ago. Why was he reading gossip rags? He put his phone away just in time for the buzzer to sound, letting them know their table was ready.

A hostess inside led the way through the crowded restaurant and out to the patio. Eric pulled out a chair for Lucy on their side of the table, and Benneck did the same for Anne. That was the moment it hit Eric hardest. He was on a double date with his ex. How did he get here?

Lucy was dying to order for everyone, sure she knew what they would like. Eric didn't mind and neither did the other two. It didn't look like it would matter. From glancing around at the other tables, the dishes coming out were beautifully-plated, tiny masterpieces. Even if the food didn't taste good, a few bites was all he'd get.

"Okay, I have to hear more about Wyatt Ellis," Lucy insisted, leaning forward to grin at Anne. "He's seriously dreamy." Lucy glanced over at Eric and rubbed his arm. "I just mean the characters he plays in his movies. You've got nothing to worry about, babe."

Oh, he had plenty to worry about, and the surprised glances from Benneck and Anne weren't helping. He hadn't even kissed Lucy, and yet he still managed to lead her on. Just more proof his instincts when it came to women were never right. Eric picked up the drink menu and flipped through the pages, though the last thing he needed was his decisions impaired by alcohol right now. He was doing fine being an idiot all on his own.

Anne twisted her napkin around her fingers. "He's like most celebrities. Very charming, with a magnetic personality, and a slightly inflated view of his own importance." She said it matter-of-factly, as if she came across famous people every day, which she sort of did.

Benneck looked thoughtful. "That sounds exactly like my dog."

Eric raised an eyebrow. "You don't have a dog."

"I did growing up. His name was Buster. Great dog. Very charming. But he didn't understand the word 'no.' I finally let him sleep in my bed with me so he'd stop whining." Benneck turned to Anne. "Lessons to be learned there, my friend."

Anne smacked his arm and her face turned an adorable shade of red. "Will you please stop?"

Lucy's laugh rang out. "You two are a riot. We have to make this a regular thing."

Eric felt like he needed air, even though he was outside with a stiff ocean breeze making them all slightly chilly. He had already given up his jacket to Lucy.

He got up and moved to the railing, looking down on the pedestrians below who were enjoying an evening walk along the beach.

"Are you okay?" Lucy asked, getting up to follow him.

"Yes. Stay and order for us. I'm just going to walk down and stick my feet in the sand for a minute." His voice came out casual and friendly, and he smiled at her before making his way down the stone steps to the beach. They were well-used and almost smooth in places from the constant foot traffic.

He didn't really intend to stick his feet in the sand. It would require taking off his socks and shoes, and he wasn't walking far enough towards the shore to get away from the cigarette butts and litter that mixed with the sand right by the sidewalk.

He shoved his hands in his pockets instead and concentrated on the crash of the waves up the beach. They were a constant thing, like the never-ending sky he so frequently cut his way through.

He stayed too long. It had only felt like a minute, but he realized it had been longer when he heard his name being called and he turned to see Lucy making her way down the steps.

"You didn't tell me what you wanted to drink," she hollered, a bright, beautiful smile on her face. She took another step and her flimsy shoe slipped from under her. Like a horrible dream, he watched her slip and hit her head on the stone steps. Then she didn't move at all. There were gasps all around as people gathered, momentarily blocking her from Eric's sight.

He ran to her, pushing bystanders aside until he could see Lucy. They didn't know her. He should be the one to help, but it already looked like several people were calling for an ambulance on their cellphones.

"Don't touch her!" one guy commanded as a woman moved to touch her neck. "She could have a spine injury."

"I have to see if she's breathing!" the woman snapped back at him.

Eric's whole body shook, and his brain felt like it was stuttering. He had to do something, he should do something, but he didn't know what that was.

Someone tugged on his arm, and he looked over to see it was Anne, coming to stand in front of him. She was holding Lucy's purse. "Go wait for the ambulance and bring them down here." Anne took off her jacket and covered Lucy's still form, before draping someone else's jacket over Lucy's legs. To help with shock, Eric's sluggish mind realized.

He sprang up the steps and weaved through tables until he reached the gate leading to the front. Unlatching it, he threw it open wide just as the blare of sirens grew closer. When the ambulance pulled to a stop, he waved the paramedics down and guided them to where Lucy was, explaining what had happened and when.

To his immense relief, Lucy had regained consciousness, though she was whimpering in pain. He watched them look her over and carefully maneuver her onto the tarp-like stretcher and carry her up the steps past a white-faced Benneck and Anne.

Lucy held up her arm from the stretcher. "Eric?"

"I'm right here." He ran over, feeling like the last person who should be comforting her, but willing to do anything she asked.

She gripped his fingers. Tears leaked out of her eyes and down the sides of her face into her hair. "Stay."

"Of course." He threw his car keys to Benneck, and with the paramedic's permission, climbed into the back of the ambulance with them.

***

Anne knew when Eric was upset, all he wanted was to be left alone, to work out his problems within the confines of his own mind. His hair stood on end from where he had run his hands through it, and all he did was pace from one end of the hall to the other, looking as tortured as she'd ever seen him. But he would be okay, and better if she didn't hover. He'd reach out when he was ready.

It was Benneck who had her worried. He was a silent piece of granite, shuttered inside himself. His hatred of hospitals was evident in every part of his body language.

Anne didn't get the luxury of either option. There were people to call and arrangements to be made. Mary had been hysterical, Lucy's parents calmly upset. They were driving up from Van Nuys now. Anne still held Lucy's purse and had filled out the intake paperwork with Lucy's insurance information.

From a phone call with Etta, she learned Lucy had a latex allergy and passed that important detail onto the nurses. Etta had sobbed in despair, knowing traffic would keep her from arriving at the hospital for at least an hour. She was sure Lucy would die before she could get there, despite Anne's reassurances that everything would be okay. Etta finally hung up and promised to drive safe.

For the first time since the accident, there was a brief lull, and Anne could sit and worry like the other two.

But within minutes, all would be in an uproar again. The Musgrove clan would begin arriving, starting with Mary and Carl, and before that happened, Anne needed to know what to do with Benneck. He had flat-out refused to leave when she hinted maybe he should go on home and wait for news, and yet being here was obviously not good for whatever demons were in his past.

She put her things down and moved to sit next to him, taking his hand. "Benneck."

He gave a small shake of his head.

"Benneck, I don't know you well enough to know what your normal is. Talk to me or I'm going to have a nurse come look at you."

That earned her a harder shake of his head. "Don't you dare."

"I was just poking the bear, so to speak."

Benneck gripped her hand. "I appreciate that. Sort of." He was quiet for several minutes before asking, "Did Eric tell you about Jenny?"

"No." Mary had said some things about a fiancée dying, but Benneck didn't need to know that, not when he was ready to talk about it.

He took his hand back and wrung his fingers together. "We met in high school and had this crazy, on-again, off-again relationship until about a year ago. She hated being long distance, and yet something always came up to make that happen. I was a pilot, she did modeling, and neither of us wanted to give it up. And then one day she showed up on my doorstep and said none of it mattered if we couldn't be together, and she asked me to marry her." He lowered his head, leaning forward and stroking the back of his neck. "Jenny was brilliant and spontaneous like that. She got me in a way no one else ever could. And I wasted so much time I could have spent with her. We had this small sliver of happiness. She got sick soon after our engagement, and the stupid doctors didn't figure out it was cancer until it was too late. She died last October."

"I'm sorry." It was such an inadequate response to his pain, but it was all she had to offer. Eric was too far away to hear their conversation, but he stopped his pacing and looked at Benneck's bowed head before locking eyes with Anne. He seemed to be looking for permission to approach or a sign that he shouldn't.

"Come," she mouthed.

He walked toward them and sat next to Benneck, who still had his head in his hands, but managed to put out a fist to bump against Eric's.

"I'm going to buy an overpriced water bottle from the machine," Benneck said, suddenly getting to his feet. "Either of you want anything?"

Anne and Eric both shook their heads.

It wasn't until the silence became this living thing between them that Anne realized Benneck probably left them together on purpose. She didn't believe for a minute Benneck had given up on his hopeless matchmaking attempt.

She looked at the seat between them, and then at Eric, who was staring at her with an unreadable expression. To her surprise, he moved over one chair and wrapped her up in a hug. Tears popped out of her eyes, and all the stress she'd been stuffing down where it couldn't mess with what had to be done came bubbling up to the surface. She sniffled and then froze, not wanting to let the wave of emotions crash land on him.

"Don't cry now, Anne. I'll think it's my fault."

"It is your fault," she choked out.

He laughed, running one hand down her hair. Being held by Eric again, even in a platonic, comforting way was like a magic salve. Except it hurt as much as it healed. He didn't pull away so she didn't either, letting her face rest against his chest until her breathing evened out. His arms only loosened when they heard footsteps approaching.

A doctor in scrubs came into the waiting area and asked, "Are the friends and family of Lucy Musgrove here?"

Benneck hurried back from the vending machine and slid into the seat next to Anne.

She raised her hand. "I'm Lucy's sister-in-law." It was close to the truth anyway. All she wanted was to know if Lucy was okay. Anne tried to read the doctor's expression, but it was impossible to tell if he had good news or bad.

He shook her hand. "I'm Dr. Cooke. I want you to know we're doing all we can. Lucy has a concussion. Any time a person loses consciousness after a head injury, it's considered a concussion. But what we were most worried about was a possible fracture, or contusion, or bleeding in the brain. We did a CT scan and there is some swelling, enough that we're going to do surgery to relieve some of the pressure. The good news is Lucy is still awake and is not showing signs of confusion, but she is a little agitated. She wants to see her boyfriend for a minute before we take her back for surgery." He looked from Eric to Benneck, waiting for one of them to identify themselves.

"That's me," Eric said quietly. His gaze turned to Anne, and it took all she had to keep the distress in her mind quiet. She didn't want him to see any reaction from her, not disappointment, not even acceptance. Obviously, he was the boyfriend. Had the two not been holding hands in the car on the way to the restaurant? And yet hearing the title was like a little twisting knife in her heart.

Eric followed the doctor back down the hall and through the double doors, nodding as the doctor reiterated the importance of only taking a minute and being calm.

"Here we go," Benneck muttered. Anne looked behind her to see Mary and Carl bursting in the doors of the emergency room.

"Anne!" Mary threw her arms around her. "What are they saying? Can we see her?"

"They're taking her back for surgery. Eric's with her, but he'll be back in a moment."

"Why Eric?" Mary exclaimed, moving as if ready to burst through the double doors and see for herself. Carl stopped her, murmuring reassurances in her ear until Mary calmed down enough to pay attention.

Anne gave them as much of an update as she could until Eric came back out and could explain more.

He seemed resigned and solemn, and he no longer looked to Anne for reassurance, or anything else. He avoided looking at her at all, if she was being honest, and her suspicion turned to confirmation the longer they moved around each other without him acknowledging her presence. Was he just too upset? She was too tired and stressed to analyze it.

He finally got Benneck to leave with him at midnight to get sleep, as they had flights in the morning that could not be cancelled without a lot of trouble.

CHAPTER 9 ♥ THE OPPOSITE OF SUSHI

"Where's my phone?" Lucy asked, suddenly in a panic. It was the third time she had asked about it in the last hour, even though her phone was right there next to her on the side table.

Eric picked it up and handed it to her, knowing she would only stare at it blankly before putting it down again. Whatever it was she thought she wanted to do with it was either too much work or too confusing for her mending brain to handle.

It was exactly what the doctor had warned about, saying agitation and confusion were totally normal, but it didn't lessen the guilt eating away at him. This was all his fault. Lucy should be back at work, not stuck here in her apartment slowly recovering.

He'd spent every free moment he could over here, because for whatever reason, Lucy had convinced herself he was her long-time boyfriend. He wasn't about to correct her, not when it was his job to keep her feeling calm and secure. It was especially important now that her parents weren't there. They had spent three weeks staying with Mary and Carl, and that was all any of them could take of each other. Now they just called and worried from home, and threatened to come back if Lucy needed them.

The problem was, no one knew how long her recovery would take. The doctors said it was different for everyone and

Lucy was on the right track. She had good days where she seemed totally normal. Today just happened to be one of the bad ones.

Etta came out of her bedroom, all done up, and came to sit next to Lucy. "Are you hungry?" she asked. "I could make you a sandwich before I go."

"Where are you going?" Lucy asked with alarm.

"Out with Hayden and his parents." Etta gave all the details again—what restaurant they were going to and when she expected to be back. It was better if Lucy didn't know she'd heard it all before.

Etta turned to look at Eric. "You sure you're okay with staying here with her?"

"Benneck said he'd come by in a bit, but even if he doesn't, we'll be fine. I'll make us something for dinner."

Etta hugged Lucy goodbye and walked out the door, her eyebrows furrowing as she glanced back at the two of them. Eric was pretty sure Etta knew he wasn't Lucy's real boyfriend, not in the normal sense of the word, but they had never discussed it. There was no point until Lucy was better. Right now, he was one of her caretakers, and that was okay.

He went to the kitchen and opened the fridge, looking for something quick and easy they'd both like. "How do you feel about soup and sandwich wraps?" he asked.

Lucy sniffed. "I'd like sushi, actually."

That was not exactly something he could whip up. "You sure?" Sometimes she said she wanted something only to turn around and ask for the exact opposite. He considered what the opposite of sushi might be. Steak and mashed potatoes?

"Why are you asking if I'm sure?" Lucy got up from her spot on the couch and came to look in the fridge with him. "Do we have sushi in here? It might be hiding behind the eggs."

Eric quickly closed the fridge, less sure Lucy remembered what sushi was. "You know what. I'll call Benneck and see if he can grab some for us."

He pulled his phone out of his pocket and stepped away from Lucy before she tried to hug him, which she frequently did when she wasn't irritated with him. It always made him feel uncomfortable, and then guilty for feeling uncomfortable.

Benneck answered on the first ring. "What can I do?" he asked.

"Lucy says she'd like sushi."

"Can you be more specific? Like California rolls? Nigiri?"

Eric looked at Lucy and decided not to ask. "Why don't you get a variety of things, and whatever she doesn't eat, we will."

"Sure thing. Anne's coming too. She hasn't seen Lucy this week and it would do them both good." There was no teasing in his voice, just a sureness that wouldn't allow for any argument. Everyone was more serious since Lucy's accident, no one more than Benneck.

Eric hung up and guided Lucy back to the couch. He picked up the remote and flipped through the channels, looking to Lucy for some sort of opinion on what she wanted to watch, even though she rarely had one these days. It was a detail that often brought Etta to tears. Lucy used to be such a TV remote hog.

He found a nature channel special on prairie dogs with a soothing narrator who spoke with an Australian accent. "This okay?" he asked.

Lucy nodded, breaking out into a slow smile. "You think you could start talking in an Australian accent like that? It's super sexy."

That would not be happening. But he smiled, glad to see glimpses of the old Lucy. "I'm afraid you're stuck with boring old me."

"I'm okay with that." She threaded her arm through his before pulling a blanket over them and settling in to watch.

With Lucy content for the moment, Eric allowed his thoughts to move to the new wrinkle in his evening. It would be good for Lucy to see Anne, but painful for him. The list of people who needed Anne more than he needed to be away from her kept growing. He didn't see a way that spending more time with Anne could end well, at least for him. But then, everything about his life right now was a mess. Less lonely than his old life, but harder, so much harder.

***

Anne braced herself for seeing Eric and Lucy together again. It was ridiculous to be jealous of someone recovering from a brain injury, but seeing Eric so gentle and patient with Lucy tugged at Anne's heart. She walked in behind Benneck, only to see the two of them snuggling together on the couch.

In her mind, she saw herself make a quick U-turn right back out of the apartment. But of course, she didn't do that. She headed straight for the kitchen with the takeout and began opening containers and transferring the food to plates.

"Come get what you want because I have no idea what anyone likes." When she and Eric were dating, he claimed to hate sushi, but his tastes could have changed.

Someone paused the TV and the three of them came in, peering over the counter at what she'd brought.

Lucy came around and gave her a big hug. "I'm so glad you're here, Anne. I've missed you."

Anne hugged her back. "How are you feeling?"

"Not too bad today." Lucy looked down and examined all the sushi items, wrinkling her nose. "You know, now that I'm looking at all this, I don't think I actually like sushi."

"There's some white rice here too," Anne offered, before glancing at the two guys. Benneck was trying hard to hide his dismay. After all, their conversation most of the way over was about how neither of them liked sushi much, especially the not-cooked variety.

Lucy shook her head. "I think I'll just have a peanut butter and jelly sandwich and a glass of milk."

"I'll make it and bring it to you," Eric offered.

Lucy smiled and returned to the couch, leaving the three of them to stare at each other, and then down at the four pieces of nigiri, which almost looked like an exotic dessert if you couldn't smell it.

"Not it," Benneck whispered, pushing the plate towards Anne.

She pushed it in Eric's direction. "Do you eat sushi now?"

"Not the raw pink kind. I'll take those vegetarian ones, though."

She slid the cucumber and avocado rolls over to him. "Eat. I'll make the PB and J for Lucy."

He looked like he wanted to protest, but someone had to eat the takeout, so he got out a fork and moved to the tiny kitchen table, quietly eating while watching her open and close cupboards in pursuit of a jar of peanut butter. Benneck had retreated to the couch, requesting peanut butter and jelly as well.

After searching every cabinet twice, she gave up and leaned across the counter, resting her head on her arms. "Do they even have peanut butter?"

"Your guess is as good as mine." She heard Eric's chair scrape against the floor and she turned to see him get up and look in the fridge. "Maybe they refrigerate it."

"What kind of weirdo—" She didn't bother finishing because he held up a jar of creamy after sifting through the contents of the door shelves. "It was behind the ketchup." He pulled out the grape jelly as well and set them both down in front of Anne where she had the bread and butter knife waiting. Instead of retreating back to the table, he stood next to her and opened both jars, his shoulder brushing against hers more often than not as he went to work making the sandwiches.

There was no logical reason why she needed to stand there with him, taking note of every time their skin touched. Love sure did make fools, and if there was any truer fact on Earth, it was that she never stopped loving Eric. They had been so young and everything happened so fast. Her own parents' marriage, and their second marriages, had been whirlwind romance disasters. Divorce was all she knew—the inevitable crash after the high of falling in love.

Breaking it off had seemed right at the time. A decision to

exclude him from her spectacle of a life and let him grow up and find out what he really wanted. Right now, standing next to him in this tiny apartment kitchen, she wished she'd been a little more willing to take a risk. What did her family know about lasting love anyway? And who were they to tell her she'd never have it?

"You okay?" Eric asked.

She looked down and saw he had the two sandwiches ready to go. He'd even cut them into triangles with the crusts off, as if he were serving toddlers.

"I'm fine. Just lost in thought."

"I'm sorry about all the leftovers. That couldn't have been cheap."

She shrugged. "I'll take it home to Carl. Mary hates sushi so he never gets it. He'll be thrilled." With that decided, she made sure everything was packaged up tightly before sticking it in the fridge.

Benneck had saved her a spot on the couch, though why they were watching a show about prairie dogs was beyond her understanding.

CHAPTER 10 ♥ IN FOR A PENNY, IN FOR A POUND

Anne's favorite days at work were when she got to do tours with Beth. Her old friend had a magical influence over the older kids Anne wished she could bottle up and sell.

Somehow, the teens instinctively knew there was something wrong with Beth, that just getting out of bed was a struggle for her, but she was thumbing her nose at her pain one day at a time. And she was funny and edgy in a way Anne couldn't hope to mimic, no matter how many times she adjusted her tour speech for the older set.

"Coming up," Beth said, "is the museum's least favorite exhibit. The spikes on the Stegosaurus tail are super authentic *and* super dangerous. The little kids take that fake mountain over there as a personal challenge to get over this glass wall in hopes of impaling themselves on a real dinosaur. We've had several staff meetings about taking off the spikes, or rounding them off, or wrapping them in bubble wrap, but like most meetings, everyone feels good about being heard and nothing gets done. Maybe drop your own suggestion in the comment box on your way out today. Let's keep moving. Please keep your cellphones out of your face so you don't fall down the stairs coming up on your left."

Anne brought up the rear, making sure no one decided to break off and have their own tour. It was less of a possibility when Beth was leading. Her deadpan delivery guaranteed no one knew when she was being serious and when she was messing with them. Several kids were filming the whole thing on their phones, staying up close so they could hear it all.

"Izzy the Isisaurus is coming up on our left. The sign posted says the slide is for ages ten and under, but I'll look the other way if anyone wants to go try it out. Don't worry about the peer pressure to stuff down your inner-child, that whole thing is going to do a one-eighty when you reach college, my friends."

Most of the kids looked confused, which only increased Beth's enjoyment, no doubt. She looked at Anne, holding up three fingers. They often took bets on how many older kids would give in to the slide's allure when Beth dared them.

Today, no one did.

When the tour ended and the last of the kids said goodbye and ran to their bus, Beth sank down onto a bench, looking older and tired. Anne sat next to her.

"You're on your feet too much."

Beth shook her head. "I can't go back to sitting at the front desk selling tickets and vouching people's parking tickets. I'd die of boredom."

"Yes, but you'd have more time for celebrity gossip. I don't even know what TMZ is saying about Wyatt Ellis today. You haven't given me my update yet."

Beth wrinkled her nose. "You mock me, and yet you're exchanging texts with a man I know more about than you do."

"You can't learn about a person from anonymous sources looking to catch you at your worst. Imagine if our lives were like that. 'An anonymous source saw Anne Elliot buying not one, but two candy bars from the overpriced vending machine in the break room today. She can't afford the calories or the extra expense, but obviously the stress of work is getting to her.'"

Beth laughed. "Okay, you may have a point there. But sources do say Wyatt Ellis has a secret girlfriend, so watch out.

You might be joking about your future in the tabloids."

"I'm not his secret girlfriend. I'm a friend of a friend, and even that's stretching things. Don't worry about me."

"I never do. Science class nerds forever." Beth held up her hand for a high five, which Anne returned, shaking her head.

Beth groaned and got to her feet. "See you tomorrow, old friend."

Anne watched her go before starting on her end-of-shift duties. It was her turn to wipe fingerprints off of all the plaques in front of the displays and make sure the life-size dinosaur puzzles still had all their pieces. When she was done, she gathered up her things from her locker and checked her phone on her way out.

Lizzie had called. That was a surprise. Anne's oldest sister reached out so infrequently, seeing her name on the missed calls list was a bit of a shock.

Anne hit the reply button on her way out, and Lizzie answered on the first ring. She was never far from her phone.

"Hey, Liz. I just got out of work. Is Dad okay?"

"Never been better. Filming just wrapped up, and he claims it's his best work ever. Don't ask about the money, though, because they paid him practically nothing. His agent is worthless, I swear. Anyway, that's not what I wanted to talk to you about."

Anne spotted her new-to-her car at the back of the museum parking lot and threaded between vehicles to reach it. "I'm listening."

"We're coming to San Francisco for a bit, just for a change of scenery. Wyatt and I have grown close these past few months and well, I think he wants us wherever he is." That last part was said with a breathy glee.

"Wyatt Ellis?" Anne asked.

"Yes, Wyatt Ellis. What other Wyatt would I be talking about?"

Anne sighed. It had been a vain hope that maybe there was another Wyatt in Lizzie's life. But it never hurt to be sure about these things, especially when it came to Lizzie's dating life.

Lizzie cycled through boyfriends at breathtaking speed.

"Okay, so how long is 'just for a bit' and where do you plan to stay?" Anne would deal with the Wyatt Ellis aspect later. Whether or not he was in a relationship with Lizzie was a secondary concern if Anne's family was about to descend on her for an unforeseen amount of time.

"Relax, Anne. I'm getting there."

One could only hope. Anne had learned long ago, if she didn't ask the right questions she never got to the point in any conversation with Lizzie.

"Did you know Wyatt owns an Aston Martin? He promised to let me drive it when we come."

"When is it you're coming?"

"Oh, as soon as we finish packing. And as for where we'll stay, I guess Wyatt has this little condo he needs someone to keep an eye on, and who better than us?"

"Who better?" Anne echoed. She would be having a text conversation with Wyatt later. She wasn't quite brave enough to call him, although she had come to expect his cryptic text messages every day. What was the guy up to now? TMZ was definitely not doing its job.

"Anyway, I just wanted to give you a heads up. Let Mary know, will ya? I'm already late for my nail appointment, and I know she'd want to talk my ear off." With that, Lizzie hung up.

Anne sighed and started up her Toyota Corolla. It had none of the frills of her last car. In fact, no matter how many times she vacuumed it, the interior still left cat hair on her from the last owner, but it ran, and her Mercedes was now someone else's problem.

Lizzie and Dad would die when they saw what she was driving, which apparently, would be soon. How soon exactly was 'as soon as we finish packing?' That could mean today or a week from today.

She drove home, and while helping the boys with their drone helicopter, relayed her conversation with Lizzie to Mary, who welcomed the news about as well as Anne had.

"What do they mean they're staying in Wyatt Ellis's condo?

Are they part of his entourage now? Are they into drugs, do you think?"

"Mary, you're going to give me an ulcer. I hadn't even considered those things. But I don't think Wyatt is a drug addict."

Mary smirked. "Why, because he texts you about his day? Because his dimples could launch their own clothing line?"

"Look, I find the situation strange as well. But I guess it will be nice to see them more often."

Mary harrumphed. "They don't exactly go out of their way to see me. And they absolutely have no patience for Colter and Charlie." Looking over at them, her eyes widened. "Boys! Not over the fence. The neighbors will threaten me with legal action again."

Colter and Charlie zoomed their drone back into the yard, letting it dangerously hover a few feet over the pool before lifting it over the fence and across the grass.

Mary groaned. "I hate that thing, but it does keep them busy. I keep hoping they'll break it. My friend Carmen absolutely assured me they would destroy the thing in a week. By the way, how is Lucy? I need to get over there and see her."

"I need to go see her, too. Last I heard, she was doing much better. She's even talking about going back to work soon. Eric and Benneck are over there a lot, keeping her company."

"There's nothing more alluring than a damsel in distress. I dare say they'll both be in love with her before long."

"She's with Eric," Anne said blandly. Maybe if she said it enough it would cease to be a shock to her system.

"Well, it's high time you were with someone, Anne. At the very least, call up Wyatt and flirt your way to some better information about Dad and Lizzie." Mary clapped her hands. "Boys! Dinner time!" Not waiting to see if they listened, she turned and went inside.

And as if Mary had planned the whole thing, Anne's phone chirped with a new text message from Wyatt.

Ready to meet up? Just got into town.

Anne sat down on the porch step and stared at her phone for

a whole minute before responding.

I got a call from Lizzie today.

You sound mad. Or your text seems aggressive. Ish. I'd actually like to see you all spun up. It's hard to picture.

Wyatt. :/ What is going on? Lizzie says she's staying in your condo here in SF.

Ok. Definite jealousy vibes going on. Which is totally unnecessary. She AND your father AND your favorite groupie, Penelope, are staying in one of my condos. I have several. Condos.

For some reason, his text conjured up images of a smiling Mr. Collins bragging about all the staircases at Rosings. She was either losing her mind or had watched the BBC Pride and Prejudice miniseries too many times. Anne pressed her phone to her forehead before typing out an answer.

Okay, but why?

Why not? Your dad and sister have become something of a second family to me, and I like getting my way. Is that so bad? We'll all have fun, I promise. I'm texting you an address. Come meet me for dessert at eight. I haven't had sugar in six months.

Well, how could she say no to that? Besides, someone had to keep an eye on her family and their new honorary member. She rolled her eyes. He liked getting his way, huh? Why was that not at all a surprise?

***

Eric taxied into the airport in San Francisco, grateful the weather had cleared enough for them to do the last leg of their flight. For a while there he thought he'd be stuck in Denver waiting out a thunderstorm. Adam, his brother-in-law, had been his copilot today, and nobody was more eager to get home than him.

The two of them worked together with single-minded focus on getting the post-flight inspection done and filling out the paperwork. The people on their flights today had been especially demanding, and he felt bad for the flight attendant who had spent her entire time fetching things for them and listening to their complaints about her when she did get to retreat to her seat.

Not every rich person was as uppity as Anne's family had been to him, but many were. It was a wonder Anne had turned out so down-to-earth. Maybe it was because, not wanting to be an outsider in her own family, she had made herself indispensable to them. It was her way of fitting in.

He'd been thinking back on their relationship more and more these days, and the grudge he'd been holding onto kept shrinking against his will. He didn't want to see Anne's side of things or consider that maybe he'd been just as hasty, running away after she returned his ring instead of fighting to keep her. But if he kept shifting the blame to himself, the regret might kill him.

He called Lucy on his way home. It was part of his routine now. She often went to bed early and he just left a message for her to listen to later, but this time she answered.

"Eric, how was today? Where did you fly to?"

He took his time answering, describing the flights and the fussy passengers. She loved all the details of what the rich and famous insisted on having on board, like the woman who brought her support iguana to hold on her lap and ordered a chopped salad for it. He was Lucy's living, breathing celebrity insider.

"Do you need me to come over?" he asked when there was a lull in the conversation. He hadn't been over in a while, and he was surprised she hadn't said anything about it.

"Oh, no. Benneck's actually on his way. It's movie night." With that, she hung up.

It's movie night? Eric put his phone on the console, both relieved and confused at her quick dismissal of him. It was good of Benneck to spend time with her. Probably good for both of them, actually.

Now he had a free night with no plans. He stopped off at a Greek restaurant with a takeout counter and got in line. They were always slammed, but the line moved quickly, and the food was worth the wait.

While debating between a kabob plate or a gyro and fries, he noticed the two women in front of him trying their best to keep their squealing under wraps as they looked at a picture on their phone.

"You're so lucky. I should have been the one to ask him."

"It's too bad they asked us to leave. He was so nice. He would have taken a photo with you, too. Stinking uppity baker."

They glanced around, as if afraid the aforementioned baker would catch them grousing.

"Are you going to post it?"

"Well, yeah. But not right now or everyone will flood the place and Wyatt will be so mad at me."

"Wyatt Ellis!" the other one squeaked before covering her mouth. They finally noticed the line had moved quite a bit, and giggling, took several steps forward.

Eric did too, telling himself it wasn't because he wanted to hear more. He really needed to stop eavesdropping on people, especially when the gossip always seemed to involve Wyatt Ellis. So the movie star was in town. Eric wondered if Anne knew and if she was one of the reasons he was here.

"Do you think that was his girlfriend with him?" one of the women whispered. "Lucky duck."

"I know. A chocolate eclair *and* Wyatt. It's like every woman's fantasy. I don't think she's a celebrity though. Not with those Walmart sandals she was wearing. I should know, I have on the same pair."

Eric looked down at the woman's feet and then quickly back up before they noticed him listening in.

"He called her Anne. Maybe it wasn't a girlfriend. We'll have to look it up and see if Wyatt has a sister with that name. Or an assistant. I bet it was his assistant."

The Greek restaurant was next door to a French pastry shop.

Was that where the women had come from? Their conversation was like a gift-wrapped invitation for him to go see. Just a quick check. He had to know if it was Anne. *His* Anne. He could never think of her another way, no matter what he told himself.

The women put in their orders, and he stepped up and ordered right after, no longer caring what he ate. As soon as he had his receipt with his order number, he turned around and went outside to walk next door.

One glance through the bakery window, and he knew his plan wasn't going to work. Half the booths were not in view, but the front counter was, and the stout woman standing behind it stared him down with her arms folded. He had mere seconds to decide. It was walk away or go inside and buy something. Hating himself a little bit, he grabbed the front door, making the bell over it jingle merrily. In for a penny, in for a pound.

He walked right up to the counter and ordered the first thing he saw: three brightly colored macarons. The woman behind the counter wrapped them carefully before sliding them into a bag and handing them to him.

His focus had stayed on her and the display counter, and it turned out he didn't need to do any strategic snooping because a male voice called out his name.

He looked over to see Wyatt Ellis leaning outside of a booth and beckoning him over. Anne had her back to him, but her body language screamed embarrassment, whether that was because she'd been caught hanging out with a movie star or because she told the movie star her ex was in the bakery, he wasn't sure. Obviously, she had to have said something, because Wyatt Ellis didn't know Eric from Adam.

He walked over to the two, and Anne slid farther into her side of the booth, giving him room to sit down. He purposely slid in closer to her than he needed to. His inner caveman was rearing its ugly head.

"Hi, Anne. I haven't run into you in a while."

"How's Lucy?" she asked, her voice slightly cool. Was she jealous?

"A little better each day. She and Benneck are hanging out

tonight." Needing something to do, he got out a macaron and took a small bite. It wasn't as dry and crumbly as he had expected, or as sweet. He liked the buttery almond flavor. It was almost worth ruining his appetite for dinner.

Wyatt Ellis studied him with a slight, knowing smile. "Any friend of Anne's is a friend of mine."

"Eric Wentworth." Eric put out a hand and shook Wyatt's.

"Wyatt Ellis. Nice to meet you. So, how do you know Anne?"

Not knowing what Anne had already said about him, Eric shrugged. "We met in college."

"Way back then. Good. That means you understand how overbearing her family can be. You should come along when I have a little get-together at my place Saturday night. I don't want her hiding in a corner while her sister hogs all the attention."

"Mary?" Eric asked.

"No, Lizzie. Have you met Lizzie?"

Eric glanced at Anne, who was blushing furiously and doing her best to pretend her flushed skin was some low acquaintance she refused to acknowledge.

"It's been a long time, but yeah, I've met Lizzie."

"Well, great! Then, come." Wyatt beamed. "I get a little Downton Abbey about having even numbers for dinner. Write your number on this card, and I'll send you the address and the gate code for the night of the party."

Anne shook her head. "I don't think—"

"I'd love to." Eric said, cutting her off. He might as well face this thing head on. Avoiding her family, avoiding their past, was not helping with his unresolved feelings. If he was going to get over her once and for all, he had to see her with them and make his heart accept the truth. She would always choose what her family wanted over her own happiness, and never even realize it.

***

What was Eric doing? Anne had been trying to think of an excuse to get out of Wyatt's little get-together, and now he was adding guests solely for her benefit. It didn't help that she couldn't seem to cool down. She felt like her shirt had shrunk three sizes since Eric walked in, and it was all she could do not to tug at her collar. He looked so incredibly attractive in his pilot uniform, something she had not been prepared for at all. It was better not to even look in his direction or she'd never stop staring.

When he made his excuses and left, she felt both better and worse.

Back to the two of them, Wyatt leaned across the booth and gave her a knowing smile. "Eric wasn't just your friend before, so what was he?"

Anne stared him down, wondering what had given her away. Not that it was any of Wyatt's business. It was better not to answer him. She had a feeling he was confident in his own conclusions without confirmation from her.

"Your silence is speaking volumes." He tapped his lips. "So, it was a romantic relationship."

She squirmed, wracking her brain for a convincing lie, but nothing came. "Yes," she finally admitted.

"And what about right now? What is he to you now?"

"He's a friend. More like a friend of a friend, to be honest. He's my platonic friend."

She'd said it more to reassure herself, but apparently Wyatt took it another way because he reached across and took her hand. "Good. And just so you know, I'm not the jealous type." He motioned towards her half-finished éclair. "Eat. You're making me feel self-conscious about the two I devoured."

It was a great excuse to withdraw her hand, despite not wanting another bite of the eclair. It was too rich and filling, even for her. Avoiding the custard middle, she took a bite off the side.

She considered telling Wyatt right then and there he had the wrong idea about the two of them, but maybe that should wait until she knew what the right idea was. A few friendly texts and one momentary handhold did not a commitment make.

There wasn't really anything particularly wrong with Wyatt except for the big disparity in their lifestyles. In fact, it made sense he would seek out someone who understood what his job was like, and yet was set apart from it. Dating other celebrities had to be exhausting.

Anne felt eyes on her, and immediately set her gooey dessert down. She looked over to see a shy fan waving at Wyatt from the bakery counter. Wyatt gave her a wink. From the way the woman fluttered, that little gesture had probably made her whole day. She walked out with her croissants in hand, practically floating.

"Does it ever get old?" Anne asked. Her father, for all his attention-seeking, had never liked interacting with fans.

"Sometimes, but it's what my job is for, isn't it? If no one recognized me or cared about me, would they come watch my films?"

She could think of several exceptions to that rule. "They would come watch you even if you were an ogre in real life, but that doesn't mean you should be one. I think it's nice to hang out with someone so ... nice."

They smiled at each other, and Anne relaxed a little. Seeing Eric had put her on edge, but their lives were moving apart again, as they should.

Except for Saturday night, her brain reminded her.

Needing something else to think about, she asked Wyatt about the movie he had just finished filming. He had all sorts of interesting stories to share, like how the director cranked up the temperature on set so their sweat would look natural, and what it was like choreographing action sequences. Those scenes were all flashbacks. Her father had played a much older version of Wyatt, languishing in a maximum-security prison cell and writing his memoirs with the help of a scrappy, young journalist.

Before getting up to leave, she tapped the table top. "Shoot. Saturday night I have a museum thing. I totally forgot. And I can tell Eric so he doesn't show up without me."

Wyatt raised one eyebrow, scrutinizing her for several

seconds. "Nice attempt, but you oversold it, honey. Actor, remember?" He took her hand up again, rubbing his thumb over her knuckles as if the sensation fascinated him. "This is your town and no one is going to run you off from hanging out with me. I want you there, isn't that enough? Don't make me beg. I'm really good at it." He gave her some pretty convincing puppy dog eyes to sell the point.

"All right, fine." She couldn't help feeling that Wyatt had brought her family here with him in some misguided attempt to bridge a gap that didn't need fixing. How could she tell him she had just escaped? Not that she didn't plan to see them at all, but at a high society party? She'd always been okay with being on the fringes, ignored, but not in such a public display.

"This is a small party, right? I don't have to show up in an evening gown or anything, do I?"

Wyatt reached out and squeezed her hand. "Very small. And I can't speak for everyone else, but I'll be in jeans."

CHAPTER 11 ♥ I DON'T BELONG HERE

Eric's phone rang as he was finishing up his last reps of sit-ups in his bedroom. He groaned and stretched before leaning across his floor and swiping his phone from the bed. It was Lucy. Their conversations this past week had been few and brief, and she never called this late at night. He quickly answered before it went to voicemail.

"Hey, Lucy. Is everything okay?" Maybe she had slept too much today and was now restless. That would make two of them. Not the oversleeping, but the restlessness, for sure. Every time he closed his eyes, Anne haunted him.

"Everything is fine, I guess. I just ... we really need to talk."

"Of course." He rested his head back against the bedspread and closed his eyes. Maybe talking to Lucy would make him tired enough to sleep.

"We need to break up."

He sat up, silently punching the air with his fist before schooling his reaction. "Whatever you want to do."

She sighed. "Benneck thought you might have that reaction. Now I owe him a Coke."

"You and Benneck talked about this?" Had Benneck convinced Lucy to let Eric go? It was so like him to interfere.

"Eric, can you be straight with me? Everything around the accident is fuzzy, but I'm starting to think some of the things I thought I forgot didn't actually happen. Like us. Did we ever … happen?"

"Define happen," he said, wanting to be very careful about upsetting her. He still wasn't sure how much had been wishful thinking on her part and how much had been his own doing, leading her on without meaning to.

"Were we a couple?"

"We were out on a date the night it happened. I don't know where it would have led if you hadn't fallen. Regardless, you're my friend and I wanted, I still want, to be there for you."

"Holy Cannoli, you've been my pity boyfriend all this time, haven't you? I'm so sorry. I release you from that. Starting now."

"Lucy, hanging around you has never been about pity."

"Well, good. I'm glad we cleared that all up. Now I have something else to confess. It's about Benneck."

And just like that, the pieces fell into place, along with a new worry. "Lucy, I told you about Benneck. He's not in a place where he can be in a relationship right now." Any more than I am.

"Oh, I know. Believe me. He told me in no uncertain terms he'll never love another woman again right before we made out on my couch tonight. Talk about mixed signals. Sorry, I know you don't want the details. Anyway, I'm okay with it. I've got nothing but time and I'm willing to take that risk. I know I can't ask him to turn off his grief any more than I can demand my brain to immediately heal. It either will or it won't."

"Then I won't lecture you anymore. Or Benneck. This is something I think he won't want to talk to me about anyway."

"I imagine not." Lucy gave a little giggle. "So, we're good?"

"Yeah, we're good."

She hung up and he tapped his phone on his knee, thinking and thinking, and not sure why everything came back to a desire to call Anne and get her opinion on Benneck and Lucy. What an unlikely pair. But he wouldn't call Anne because on the fringes of that conversation would be the murky water of how he'd ended up as Lucy's boyfriend in the first place, and why Anne was the first person he thought to call and tell.

The only reason he still planned to go to Wyatt Ellis's little dinner party on Saturday night was because it was a ready-made excuse to see Anne. Oh, he had all these noble pretexts about trying to get over her. It was still his deepest wish, the most sensible thing if he wanted to keep his dignity or his heart intact, but underneath the logic was the simple craving to be around her. That never went away.

And now he was a free man to boot. Lucy had cut him loose.

His elation was quickly tempered by caution, though maybe it was too late for that. He doubted Anne thought about him at all, compared to how often he thought about her. Here he was spiraling down the same whirlpool of romantic misery, and of his own free will.

He pressed his palms together. No matter what, he wouldn't do anything stupid, anything that would reveal his feelings for Anne unless she took the leap first. In that, he'd be safe. Anne would never throw herself at him, especially not in front of her family and their celebrity friends.

***

After Anne finally finished trying on different outfits and doing her hair, she felt like collapsing on the bed in a heap. Trying to appear confident, yet casual took too much work. But if there was even the smallest chance Eric would show up tonight, Anne had to be prepared. Mostly because the thought of him in the same room as her father and sister again was enough to make her want to hide under her covers and pretend to be sick. She likely would be sick if she dwelled too much on it. It was better if she focused on the task at hand, which at the moment, was carefully applying mascara and taking deep, slow breaths to ward off anxiety.

"Hello!" Mary called out. She came bustling back to Anne's bedroom, dropping Anne's jean jacket unceremoniously on the bed as if a trip out to the guest house was merely a walk down the hall to a bedroom.

"You left this on the hook by the front door," Mary said, stopping to take in Anne's look. "That's more makeup than you usually wear."

"You and Carl are sure you don't want to come?" Anne asked. As much of a kill-joy as Mary often was, she was also familiar and dear. Mary would never ditch her at a party for someone more exciting.

Mary wrinkled her nose. "Of course, I'm sure. Our invitation was an afterthought. I wouldn't dream of accepting. How humiliating would that be? Besides, we have to go to Lizzie's don't-mention-it's-her-birthday brunch on Monday."

"I forgot about that. Am I supposed to bring a gift?"

Mary wagged her finger. "You should always have one just in case. You never know with her. How despondent will she be to be turning thirty-four, do you think?"

Anne shrugged. "Well, all I have is a cat sweater anyway. I'll put it in a gift bag and put it in front of Beauregard. Can't go wrong there."

Mary laughed. "Except she's told you a million times to stop making those ugly sweaters."

"I choose not to hear it."

Mary came over, running a hand through Anne's carefully crafted beach waves before holding out her hand for the curling iron. "There's a spot back here."

Anne handed Mary the wand and held still while she fixed the back and tousled it. "So, does this mean you and Wyatt actually have a thing going on? Because I know you stopped trying to dress up for Dad's benefit a long time ago. And good riddance, too, right?" Mary wrinkled her nose. "One time, I wiped olive oil across my nose and sat down right next to him with a bag of potato chips. I dug my hand as deep in as it would go and pulled out a handful of chips to eat in one bite. I thought he was going to have a stroke. You would think I had lit up a cigarette and blown smoke in his face the way he went on and on about how I was destroying my body and his respect for me."

Anne laughed. "He does like to say you're the reason he had to start dying his hair so early."

Mary's eyes narrowed. "But about Wyatt, don't let this go too far, okay? Don't move into his condo or anything."

"As if. I only mooch off you, dear Mary."

"You pay rent, and you watch my boys for free, which no one else would ever agree to. Do you know what the little monsters did this morning?"

Anne shook her head, watching her hair bounce in the reflection. She needed to do her hair like this more often.

"In an attempt to one-up Colter in hide-and-go-seek, Charlie cut his bean bag chair open and climbed inside. And then when Colter found him, the two picked up the thing and shook it like a bottle of soda until it rained foam beads all over their room."

Anne had been trying not to laugh, but Mary's exasperated reflection in the mirror warning Anne not to find it funny was what finally did her in. She laughed so hard she almost cried. Almost. The thought of redoing her eye makeup sobered her up quickly.

"Anyways, Carl is helping them clean up the mess now. I'd better go and supervise. Text me if anything interesting happens, okay? You won't remember it exactly if you wait to tell me tomorrow." With a little wave, she left, closing the front door firmly behind her.

Anne smiled. Did Mary think she had the memory recall of a hamster? Although, it had been nice of Mary to fix her hair. It was now a little bigger than she preferred so Anne smoothed it down a little before locking up and going out to her car.

Wyatt's home was in the ritzy sea cliff area of San Francisco, and the outside of the gigantic house did not disappoint with its bright white columns, arch windows, perfectly manicured hedges, and warm garden lights guiding her way up the steps to the front door. Several cars were parked outside the gate, but she wasn't prepared for the sheer number of people inside, mingling around behind Penelope, who had opened the front door the second she knocked.

"Oh, hello," Anne said. Penelope looked as fabulous as always in some sort of intricate wrap dress, but she wore a deep frown, which was not like her at all. Penelope always appeared pleased with everything.

"Welcome to the party," Penelope said, gesturing for Anne to come inside.

Anne walked in and turned to see Penelope close the door after her and stay there, hands behind her back, like a butler.

She didn't have time to dwell on it because Wyatt emerged from the crowd and smiled big. "Just the person I've been waiting for." He took Anne's arm, calling over his shoulder, "Thank you, Penelope. You've been such a big help."

Anne didn't dare look back to see Penelope's reaction. "What did you do to her?" Anne hissed at him.

He only laughed. "Your family got here early, and Penelope asked if there was anything she could do to help. So, I took her up on it."

"I bet she'll never make that mistake again," Anne said, dodging around a cackling woman with a precariously held wine glass. If Anne wasn't mistaken, it was Tony award winning... somebody. The name eluded her.

Wyatt tucked Anne's arm in closer. "It wasn't the nicest thing to do. But it's already served its purpose. Penelope's away from your father, allowing him to mingle a bit without the arm candy."

Anne glanced around until she spotted her father chatting with a trio of beautiful people. He practically glowed with enthusiasm, or perhaps blush and bronzer. She wouldn't put it past him to do whatever it took to make his skin look its best.

"I thought this was supposed to be a small party." She thought of the few cars parked outside. Uber and Lyft must have been busy tonight.

Wyatt gave her a smile that was half apology, half mischief.

"What can I say? Everyone RSVP'd yes. Dinner is out on the balcony so it won't feel so cramped. You have to go see my million-dollar view. The maze of steps down to the beach is my favorite thing about this property."

"Okay, I think I will." Anne retrieved her arm and headed out to the back patio, leaving Wyatt to mingle with his other guests. The sound of the waves crashing against the rocks immediately soothed her nerves. She didn't belong among the rich and the hopeful, but the thought didn't make her sad anymore.

***

I don't belong here. Eric stood taller, looking over heads and around shoulders. At this point, he wasn't even trying to disguise his search for Anne. She was the reason he was here. Wyatt had asked Eric to look after her, so that's what he'd do, if she let him. Maybe he'd find her and she'd be fine. Maybe this was her life—parties and beautiful people and being seen. Somehow, he didn't think so. Not anymore. He had to hope, or else why was he here at all?

He edged around a group of people crowding a waiter with cocktails and headed for the glass patio doors. Unless Anne was hiding in a bathroom, she had to be outside. Her car parked out front was a pretty good indication that she was somewhere, and thankfully, it wasn't next to Wyatt Ellis. He was chatting with an older man wearing an orange suede sports jacket. The expensive cut elevated him from used-car salesman to eccentric rich dude.

Outside, beautiful tables were decorated with white china dishes and gleaming silverware. They must have anticipated the wind because the centerpieces were filled with crystal gems instead of flowers, and nothing so much as fluttered from the table, not even the linen napkins. He picked up one and noted the weights sewed into each corner. Ingenious.

An attendant eyed him suspiciously, and after he carefully

refolded the napkin, he looked back to see the attendant dart over and adjust it to her satisfaction. Even she saw him as an interloper.

Several people looked out over the deck down at the beach, and he joined them, watching two yachts cut through the water, leaving a white trail behind them.

The stairs leading down the beach below were an intricate zigzag that would have drawn him in before Lucy's fall. He almost turned away before he saw a lone figure standing on the bottom step. Anne. She looked like a figure out of a painting with her hair and dress tossing in the wind, showing off her natural beauty. The surf hadn't reached her yet, but it would within minutes. What was she doing?

It must be mesmerizing to watch the beach disappear and be swallowed up by the sea, but the steps would be wet and slippery, especially on the return climb.

Without any hesitation he turned and started down, being careful but quick. She was coming up as he got to the last bend, and not wanting to startle her, he called out, "Anne."

She glanced up, and her surprise turned into a self-conscious grin. She hollered something to him, but the wind flung her words away. When she was closer, she tried again. "I couldn't help myself. There are too many people up there and not enough of them that I have any claim to talk to."

"Well, that makes two of us." He held his hand out to help her up to the step he was on, and she took it without hesitation. Her hand was smooth and cold and perfect, but he didn't want to push his luck, so he let go when she reached him. He looked down at her sturdy sandals, grateful she hadn't made the trek in heels. Of course, Anne would be too practical for that.

"What's the matter?" she asked, looking down at her shoes as well. "They're not the sexiest things but they are comfortable."

Eric laughed. "You have no idea how happy I am about that. I have a complex about beach steps now. You about gave me a heart attack when I saw you down here."

"Oh, right." She tucked a wayward strand of hair behind

her ear, but the wind pulled it back out to play with. "I didn't even think about that. Sorry to make you nervous."

It was then he remembered she didn't know about Lucy and Benneck. "About Lucy..." He wasn't sure how to say it without sounding like he was announcing his newly single status. "She and I... she's decided to pursue Benneck, and I think she might actually catch him."

Anne mistook his discomfort for heartache. Pity was written all over her face. "Oh, Eric. I'm so sorry."

"Don't be. I'm fine."

She didn't look like she believed him, but he hesitated to correct her, not sure if he should.

"This won't ruin your friendship with Benneck, will it?"

"Not at all." He looked into her earnest face and the rest of it came tumbling out. "Lucy and I were never really together."

Anne cocked her head. "I'm not sure she would agree with you there."

"I know, and that's my fault. I didn't mean to lead her on. I was fine with being friends and then Etta got back together with Hayden and it was just the two of us and..."

"And things happen." Anne narrowed her eyes at him. He wished he saw more jealousy there and less teasing, but talking to her about this at all was a huge weight off his shoulders. Anne had always been the perfect confidant.

"No. It wasn't like that. I never even kissed Lucy. When she asked for her boyfriend at the hospital... there was nothing for it but to assume she meant me. It wasn't exactly the time to have a define-the-relationship discussion, so I just went with it. She needed me."

"And how does Benneck fit into all this?"

Eric threw up his hands. "I have no idea, though he once joked he would do me a favor and seduce her away from me."

"Seduce!" Anne slapped his chest. "Men! You're the worst."

"It was a joke. At least, I thought it was."

Anne tried not to laugh. "That's terrible. All out of the goodness of his heart, no doubt. I'd be more worried if I didn't know Benneck so well. He wouldn't toy with her."

"No, he wouldn't. But that doesn't mean I'm not worried." Eric fell in step with her as they climbed back up, using his nervousness about the steps and the wind chill as an excuse to tuck her in close to him. "I've called him a couple times, but he won't talk to me about her yet. He says he will when he's ready. That to me is a pretty good indication he doesn't have this figured out. Usually, no one likes to talk about their feelings more than Benneck."

Anne shook her head. "Well, I'll make him talk to me. I can't believe it. Benneck and Lucy. Do you see those two together long?"

"Wow. You're more of a pessimist than I am, Anne."

One side of her mouth curled up. "He's the one who told me he planned to be alone the rest of his life."

"I don't believe that about him anymore. Not after he met you."

"Me?" Anne stopped and turned to stare at him. "There was never anything romantic between Benneck and me. You know that, right?"

"I know. But you changed him. You change everything, Anne." His arm around her waist hadn't felt like much of a gesture until their gazes tangled for longer and longer. She was so beautiful with the wind tossing her hair around and her eyes so bright.

"Anne!"

From up above, Wyatt waved before jogging down to meet them. "I've been looking for you two all over. I should've known you wouldn't be able to resist my backyard. Isn't it beautiful?" With a casual confidence, he took Anne's arm and led her up the rest of the way, leaving Eric to follow behind.

***

Anne did not want to return to the party, but smiled and chatted with Wyatt as if she did. She was his guest after all, and she didn't want to seem unappreciative. The trip up the beach stairs was a lot harder than the trip down. Her thighs were burning by the time they reached the top step, and she was out of breath. Mary had a stair stepper in her home gym. Anne would totally be adding it to her workout regimen after this.

Wyatt grinned at her. His eyes missed nothing. "Go ahead and breathe deep. It's quite the climb if you're not used to it."

She leaned over, resting her hands on her thighs, and took a deep breath in and out, not even minding that it made both Wyatt and Eric laugh. She felt lighter after talking to Eric, full of a buzzy joy that was only dimmed by the thought of all the careful mingling ahead tonight.

Most of the guests were already seated for dinner. Attendants flitted around getting drink orders. Wyatt led her to an open spot next to him, at the same table as her father and Lizzie and Penelope. For a moment, she was relieved when Eric chose a different table, but that was followed by deep disappointment so acute it physically hurt. Was he still determined to avoid her family? There was no other reason for it, considering the open spot next to her that shone like a beacon, though logic told her no one else noticed. The seat wasn't claimed until the last guest sat down, a friend of Wyatt's who came straight from work.

"You must be Anne," the man said, putting out a hand for Anne to shake. "I'm Colin Wallis."

She shook his hand. "Nice to meet you. Do you know my father or something?"

"Not at all. I'm not in the movie business. I'm actually Wyatt's financial advisor and poker buddy. You wouldn't think those two things would go together, but in our case they do. He's mentioned you quite a lot."

Wyatt leaned over. "Colin, are you trying to embarrass me? It won't work."

Anne glanced between the two men, almost convinced they had planned this in an attempt to embarrass her. Why would Wyatt mention her to a poker buddy? Or a financial advisor?

"Wyatt." Lizzie waved her hand at him, making her bracelet bounce. "Wyatt, this hard raspberry lemonade is divine. I have to remind myself to sip or I'll be dancing on the tables before dinner comes out." She winked at him and shook the ice in her glass.

"Let's be sure to top that glass off then." He put his hand up and snapped. "Waiter."

Lizzie giggled. "Stop that."

Anne used the momentary interruption to check on Eric. He was happily chatting with the people at his table, and she was able to stare for longer than she should, since he was taking no notice of her whatsoever. He laughed at something the woman seated next to him said. It was a genuine laugh, crinkling the laugh lines at the corners of his eyes. Good. At least he was enjoying himself. Eric had never liked parties, which was why it was such a surprise when he agreed to come to this one.

"What would you like to drink, Miss?" Anne's view was blocked by a waiter in a black apron, and she looked up and fixed on an appreciative smile.

"Sprite, please."

"Be sure to bring it in a kiddie cup," Lizzie quipped.

Next to her, Penelope tittered. When Anne locked eyes with her, Penelope's eyes held a challenge in them that had never been there before. Was it because she was more secure in her place in their family? Perhaps she was annoyed on Lizzie's behalf that Anne was the one sitting next to Wyatt.

Wyatt put his arm around Anne. "Actually, that sounds nice. Will you bring me a Shirley Temple?"

"Right away, sir." The waitress hurried off.

"A Shirley Temple?" Anne asked him.

"It's just Sprite with a little bit of grenadine and a maraschino cherry."

Anne raised an eyebrow. "I know what a Shirley Temple is. I used to drink them at my father's parties when I was little."

"I'm feeling nostalgic," Wyatt said with a shrug. "I also had three beers during the mingling portion of the party, and as much as I'll enjoy watching Lizzie dance on top of the table, I'd rather not join her."

Lizzie laughed in delight, but Anne noticed Penelope's eyes narrowed on Wyatt before she smiled and joined Lizzie in her mirth. That was fair. After all, Wyatt had turned Penelope into the door greeter for the beginning half of the evening.

"Excellent party, Ellis." Anne's father, who had been in a deep, quiet discussion with the woman on his left about the merits and drawbacks of plastic surgery, picked up his drink and held it up. Everyone else at the table followed suit. Anne used her water glass.

"To Wyatt," they murmured.

"Thank you, Walter. I'm honored to be in such good company." Wyatt's smile lost a little of its brilliance as Penelope took that moment to lean in to Anne's father, who was sitting next to her, and nuzzle her nose against his ear. She whispered something that made him laugh.

It was worse than Anne thought. Out in public like this? Was it official then? What if he was buying her things? And with what money? The waiter came back with Anne's drink, and she took a small sip before going back to fiddling with her napkin. She wanted the night to be over. No, more than that, she wanted to go back to standing on the steps with Eric, to finish their conversation. The contrast between then and now was so stark, the difference between perfect comfort and sitting on edge. What had Eric meant when he said she changed everything? Right now, she felt powerless, like a tumbleweed with roots so shallow a strong breeze would send her flying.

She looked up and saw Eric watching her from his table. He smiled and held up his drink, a glass of water, if she wasn't mistaken. He'd always said Sprite was disgusting but would take a sip of hers "just to make sure." The little memory sent a flood of them tumbling into her mind, free from the confines where she usually kept them.

This time, she didn't push them away. She smiled and remembered the good times, like on her birthday when he brought her a chocolate cake which she promptly dropped on the kitchen floor after almost tripping on a pair of shoes. Their relationship had been brand new, and she'd stood there frozen in mortification, not knowing what to do. He'd frantically opened every cupboard looking for ingredients to remake it, and only stopped when she tugged on his shirt, bringing him back to her. Her heart began to pound just as it had then, because the memory of that kiss... She would never forget it. It was their first real kiss, full of passion and wonder... and laughter. They'd gotten so enthusiastic they stepped in the cake.

***

There were some interesting characters at Eric's table, there was no denying it. They were almost distracting enough to make Eric forget Wyatt's unspoken, yet unmistakable direction to sit here and not next to Anne. But why?

Speculation was such an untrustworthy source of information. Had Wyatt been putting Eric in his place or simply suggesting a friendly table for him? Maybe he knew Anne's family wasn't the easiest to make small talk with. Or perhaps he had been saving the seat for his friend who eventually came and sat next to Anne. None of it really mattered, except Eric didn't know Wyatt's intentions toward Anne. Wyatt was a persuasive man, and Anne, at least in the past, was the easily persuadable type. What was she now? He had to believe things were different.

"This is instant pudding if I've ever tasted it," the woman next to him said, dramatically setting down her spoon. "Custard indeed. And all these Easter egg colors are so insipid. It's a shame after such a delicious meal." She tsked. "I took such beautiful pictures, too. Maybe I won't mention the dessert at all."

"Are you a reporter?" Eric asked.

The man sitting on her other side scoffed. "She's a wanna-be food critic. Aren't you, Gladys?"

"Keep shoveling in that pudding, Dennis. It's what you do

best."

Eric exchanged smiles with the rest of the table. They had all been watching the couple's verbal sparring match ignite and burn out several times in the past half-hour. It hadn't ever reached food-fight status, which was a disappointment.

When the two went back to silently loathing each other, Eric looked over to see how Anne was faring. Apparently, she didn't like the custard any more than Gladys did. She picked at her uneaten dessert while Wyatt talked nonstop, his animated hands flying as he told a story.

The party was almost over. Eric debated whether to leave as soon as possible or wait Anne out in hopes of talking to her again. This war over his heart was supposed to get resolved tonight, not burn brighter. How had he ever thought seeing more of her would cure him? The magnetic pull he felt had only grown in intensity. Caution had taken a backseat to what his instincts said to do.

The vacant seat next to Anne beckoned to him. Wyatt's friend, the one who had been sitting on the other side of Anne, had made excuses and left several minutes ago. It was now or never. If Eric was about to die a social death, it wouldn't be because of cowardice.

Taking his water glass, Eric said his goodbyes to the people at his table and then walked to Anne. She had taken to swirling the custard in her crystal goblet with a spoon. Not being chocolate, it wouldn't interest her.

"What flavor was yours?" he asked quietly as he sat down.

She startled so badly she overturned the crystal goblet, only righting it at the last second by grabbing the stem. The spoon, however, clattered and spun before landing on the table cloth and splattering yellow cream everywhere.

Wyatt stopped mid-sentence, took in the sight, and smiled. "Eric, you decided to join us. Good for you. Everyone, let me introduce you to Eric Wentworth, Anne's old friend."

Eric met Anne's father's sharp gaze head on. "Nice to see you again, Mr. Elliot."

The old man gave him a nod. "Nice to see you."

Anne's sister, Lizzie, looked between Anne and Eric, obviously trying to place him in her memory. "Am I supposed to remember you?" she asked. She turned to her father. "Who is he?"

"Nobody to us now. He's the boy Anne wanted to marry when she was seventeen. Ridiculous idea. We talked her out of it quickly." He probably thought he was keeping his voice low, but the whole table heard him.

"I wasn't seventeen." Anne's voice was firm, but shaky.

"Okay, how old were you?" her father responded, calm as could be.

"Twenty."

"So I was off by three years. I guess that must seem like a lot when you're so young." He turned to laugh with the young woman at his right as she ran her hand over his arm in a way that made it very clear what kind of relationship they had. There was a lot more than three years between them, perhaps even three decades. Ah, the life of a celebrity.

Eric almost felt bad for Anne's napkin, the way she was wringing it in her hands as if trying to murder it, but he wasn't sure if she wanted him to back off or back her up, so he said nothing. Maybe coming to the table had been a mistake. The last thing he wanted was to embarrass Anne in front of her family and friends. Was she embarrassed by him? By the past?

Wyatt, never one to let a situation or conversation go on without him, was the one who ended up comforting Anne. He leaned over, wrapping his arm around her. "I love your dad, but he's never been one for tact. Sorry about your dessert, Anne. Next time just say you don't like custard."

Her responding laugh was half cry. Wyatt pulled her head against his chest, turning to look at Eric as if all of this was his fault. There was a little bit of smug triumph there too. So, that's how things were. Eric had another enemy at the table, apparently.

At least Eric finally knew where he stood with the guy. Wyatt viewed him as competition, and in his world, you brought the competition in to watch their own defeat. But Anne was not a prize to be won. If Wyatt didn't understand that, he didn't deserve her. No one here did.

The old Eric would have fought back against the injustice of it all, made a mess, picked a fight he couldn't win, only to run away and leave Anne to pick up the pieces. Not tonight. Not unless this was the future Anne wanted for herself, one where people were measured and found wanting unless they kept their masks of perfection in place. If she rejected him a second time, he would accept his fate as the fool who got told twice and let her go in peace.

Eric turned to Lizzie, knowing if there was anything that would warm Anne's sister up to him, it was talking about herself.

"Is that one of your own pieces?" he asked, pointing to the chunky white bracelet on her wrist. "You used to design jewelry, didn't you?"

She gave him a surprised smile of pleasure. "I can't believe you remember that. It was just a hobby. But, yes, this is one of my signature pieces. I like my jewelry to be big and bold, and it's so hard to find what I'm looking for. I wear it too much, but it's just fabulous, isn't it?"

"It's very bold," he said in response, taking her wrist when she held it out and examining the bracelet closer.

It was enough of an icebreaker that she kept going, telling him who else had worn her jewelry and how everyone wished she still had her accessory line. He had a feeling there was more to the story than she was sharing, something that probably involved financial trouble, but that was none of his business. He was just attempting to defuse the tension at the table.

"Anne says you have a cat named Beauregard."

"Oh, yes. He's my sweet darling," Lizzie gushed. She pulled out her phone to show him pictures, most of which had been altered on Snapchat so the cat wore a flower crown or eye glasses or other nonsense which didn't make it look any less like a goblin. Benneck would be so jealous.

A waiter came and took away Lizzie's empty dessert goblet, and she asked for coffee, giving Eric a chance to steal a glance at

Anne.

She met his gaze, and the look of gratitude Anne threw him made him feel self-conscious and more pleased than he wanted to admit. Yes, he'd done it for her, but also for him. He wanted to make amends with her family, at least enough that they could all be in the same room together without a soap opera erupting. Maybe with her father that would be impossible. At the moment, the man was too wrapped up with his date to notice anyone else. Eric, however, did not miss the way the woman continued to sneak glances at Wyatt Ellis. What twisted mess was this?

Lizzie grabbed his arm, wanting to point out a woman who had once been in a movie with her father. He listened to her story which meandered down some interesting side roads before getting to the main point, which was that Lizzie never forgot a face. Well, except his, but Eric didn't point that out.

Lizzie opened her sparkly purse and pulled out a tiny notebook. "I'm having a brunch get-together at eleven on Monday, and you should come. This is the address." She wrote it down and handed him the paper.

"I'd love to, but I'll be working. I'm sorry. Otherwise I'd be there." He wasn't sure who could be at an event in the middle of a workday.

She shrugged. "Another time."

He tucked the little paper in his shirt pocket, touched she would even offer.

A few people lingered at the tables for coffee, but many were getting up and leaving. After chatting for a few more minutes with Lizzie, Eric decided he was ready as well. Better to leave on a high note. He got up and thanked Wyatt for the party. Then he leaned down and kissed Anne's cheek as her arms came up to hug him goodbye.

"Won't you stay a little bit longer?" she whispered.

He hesitated, until he looked down to see Wyatt's hand resting comfortably on Anne's thigh. He'd misread everything. "No, I'd better go."

CHAPTER 12 ♥ PENNYWISE CHARITYPOOR

Anne had been so focused on Eric, she hadn't noticed Wyatt touching her until Eric did. And oh, did Eric notice. He was there and gone before she could even react. Anne slapped Wyatt's hand off her thigh, which would have been an inappropriate liberty even if she had been his date.

"What are you doing?" she asked.

Wyatt shrugged in a devil-may-care way. "I like you, Anne. I thought that was obvious."

"I'm sorry. I don't feel the same way." She fled from the table, weaving through people, hoping to catch Eric before he got to his car. She had no idea what she would say to him, but anything would be better than nothing.

She had to try. Even if her family had been rude. Even if he was getting over his feelings for Lucy. Even if hoping for a second chance was nothing more than a vain wish.

But Eric was gone, and she couldn't go after him because she'd left her purse on the back of her chair at the table where she'd left Wyatt sitting. She closed her eyes. What a disaster this night had turned out to be.

She took the long way through the galley kitchen to the back door, apologizing to the catering staff when she almost tripped a waiter with a tray full of dishes, and then weaving around guests to avoid Wyatt seeing her. Once outside, she slunk down, grabbed her purse, and routed a path back to the front door. It felt like a stress dream, the kind where you run and run and never make any progress.

And just like in a bad dream, she ran into the one person she hoped to avoid. Wyatt stopped in front of her, all contrition and charm, from his apologetic smile to his hands clasped in front of him, as if ready to beg for her forgiveness.

"Anne, I owe you an apology. I sometimes like to tease too much, and I'm sorry if I assumed you'd be okay with it. I need someone like you in my life. Please say we can still be friends."

"Of course." And she mostly meant it. She would be friendly, but from a careful distance from now on. She had a feeling Wyatt didn't really have friends. He had people he liked to have around and organize according to his whims, and he was always pleasant, but true friends could let their guard down. Who the real Wyatt Ellis was would remain a mystery—one she was no longer interested in seeking out.

"I'm so glad to hear that." He pulled her in for a hug which went on for too long, with him rubbing his hands across her back in a way that brought back all the discomfort of a few minutes ago. She pressed against his chest to separate them and noticed her father and Penelope coming up. She couldn't be hampered by another conversation that would keep her from getting out of here.

"Bye, Wyatt." She ducked around him and made for the front door, not stopping until she was inside her car with the door locked.

There would be no more celebrity parties. Not for her. Anne took a deep breath for the first time in several minutes and scrambled for her phone at the bottom of her purse, fully intending to call Eric and… and what? Tell him Wyatt's hand on her thigh had been a mistake? It was ridiculous to feel responsible for it, and yet she sort of did. She had let Wyatt decide the direction of their relationship up to this point, going along with whatever he initiated. And why? Because Wyatt was famous? Because he was friends with Dad? Neither of those were good reasons.

She stared at her phone, realizing with disgust that she had Wyatt as a contact, with a long, meaningless text message thread going back daily for the past month, and she didn't even have Eric's number. She had deleted it a long time ago after staring at it longingly for years.

There was nothing for it. She dialed Benneck and waited for him to answer. When it went to voicemail she hung up and texted him.

I need Eric's number ASAP.

She turned the key in the ignition, filled with gratitude that it started up with an even hum, and she drove home. Maybe someday she wouldn't expect car trouble every time she drove.

Once parked, she snuck around back, hopping over the various toys in the yard from the boys and made it to the guest house.

She opened the door, intending to throw her purse on the side table, and gave a little scream to see Mary standing there, like a robot just awakened with a motion sensor.

"Mary, you scared me to death. What are you doing?"

Mary waved her phone at Anne. "Do you not check your messages? I've been texting you all night. I was trying to be polite and not call you and interrupt… whatever. I wouldn't know since you never answered my texts."

Anne did not want to admit she had been purposely ignoring Mary's messages. Not that she planned to ignore them forever, but tonight, absolutely. There were too many other important things to worry about at the moment.

Mary read it all in her face. "I'm going to choose not to be offended right now, because I have to talk to somebody about what I found, and you're it. Congratulations. But first, what happened with Wyatt tonight?"

"Why do you think something happened?" Anne asked, feeling paranoid and frazzled, and as if everything that happened tonight was part of a conspiracy to make her lose her mind. Why wouldn't Benneck text back? He always texted back.

"I meant, how did Wyatt act with Lizzie and Dad, and that

trollop, Penelope, who hangs out with them?"

"He acted friendly, like he always does. Well, not with Penelope. He can't stand her either."

Mary wagged her finger. "That is all very interesting, and I'll show you why. Come see this interview I found on Twitter."

"An interview on Twitter?"

"Don't be a snob right now, Anne. I have precious little time between when my kids go to bed and when I go to bed, and how I spend it is my business." Mary walked back to Anne's bedroom and pushed aside the yearbook she'd brought with her to make room for them to sit on the end of the bed. Mary had obviously made herself comfortable while waiting for Anne. And had she vacuumed? There were vacuum lines in the carpet, and Anne noticed her books on the bookshelf had been rearranged by size, with some turned on their sides to make interesting patterns. It was better not to ask.

When Anne sat down next to her, Mary continued. "So, there's this interview game that's gaining popularity. It's called 'Ten Tweet Spill It.'" It's how people find out all the little dirty secrets of celebrities. Wyatt's ex-girlfriend, who's a makeup artist and huge on Instagram and everywhere, she said there's this woman Wyatt is obsessed with, though he'll deny it to his dying day. He tracks her whereabouts, and they talk on the phone and attempt to make each other jealous. She thinks they secretly meet up, too. She didn't know her name but she's sure it's someone who went to high school with him. And everyone wants to know who she is, but Wyatt guards his phone something fierce and they use fake names when they talk to each other." Mary looked up, her eyes glowing with excitement. "So, I pulled out my old yearbook."

Anne held up her hand to stop her at this point. "Mary, I'm so tired. I promise I'll go down this rabbit hole with you tomorrow, but I really need to... Do you happen to have Eric Wentworth's phone number?"

Mary wrinkled her nose. "No. Ask Lucy or Etta for that."

Of course. Anne immediately sent off a text to Etta, not wanting to ask Lucy with the whole Benneck and Eric mess.

Perhaps it was messier than Eric said and he hadn't wanted Anne to worry. Maybe he had only been eager to leave tonight and wasn't jealous at all. Self-doubt colored over everything she thought she knew, painting it in a new light.

She looked up from her phone to see Mary eyeing her curiously. "I want to know all about why you want Eric Wentworth's number, but you have to listen to me right now. I know who Wyatt's obsessed with. I know who his secret girlfriend is."

Anne put her head in her hands. "My work friend, Beth, thinks it's me. That they're talking about me. I really hope that's not true."

Mary laughed. "It's not you, dear. Don't worry."

"Well, it's not Lizzie. They both claim to be friends but they don't pay any attention to each other when they're together." Even as she said it, it sounded to her own ears like proof something sneaky was going on. Heaven forbid. "I'm sure you could find all sorts of claims about Wyatt on the internet, most of it made up. I don't think he has a secret girlfriend at all."

Mary shook her head. "Oh, he does. And it's Penelope. It explains everything. Why Wyatt put them all up in his condo. Why he's been paying you all this attention suddenly. You're the perfect person to make Penelope insanely jealous while she toys with Dad to irritate Wyatt. It's all part of the game the two of them play. It makes their relationship more exciting."

Anne stared at her, startled to realize all the nonsense Mary had been spouting since Anne walked in didn't sound like nonsense at all. "Okay, start over. I'm listening."

Mary pressed on Anne's hand. "You're not the only one who worries when Dad starts dating someone half his age. And then when Lizzie said they were staying as guests in Wyatt's condo with an open invitation to stay as long as they liked... No one in Hollywood does things like that without some kind of motive. My years of watching True Hollywood Crime were finally going to pay off. Who better than me to solve a mystery like this?"

"Who better?" Anne echoed, amused to see the little ways Lizzie and Mary were alike, despite how often the two of them butted heads.

Mary cracked open the yearbook she'd brought. "I was two years behind Lizzie and Wyatt, so they're seniors in here, but look at this group photo. Look at these two in the background."

Anne looked closer. The image was grainy, and there was nothing definitive, but it sure did look like a young Wyatt and Penelope slinking off together, both glancing back to see if anyone noticed them.

"We can't say for sure it's them."

Mary waved her arms. "That's not all. He was dating Ambrose J'ouvert at the time this photo was taken. She was a prima ballerina, more stuck up than he was. They had a huge fight after a pep assembly like a month later. She accused him of cheating on her with Pennywise Charitypoor. We all thought at the time she was referring to some girl at a public school he hooked up with on the weekends, and she was calling the poor girl, 'It,' like the horror movie clown. It was all really clever and mean and most of us sided with Ambrose because she was just that intimidating. But think about it. Pennywise. Penny. *Penelope.* I think she wanted Wyatt to know she knew exactly who it was, but she didn't want to call her out by name because it would have elevated Penelope's status at school. She was a scholarship student, and no one ever let her forget it. Not even Lizzie."

"How do you remember all this?" Anne asked.

"Why wouldn't I?" Mary shrugged. The woman did hold notorious grudges. It took a certain amount of attention to detail and an unwillingness to forget anything to hold a good grudge.

Anne's phone chirped with a return text from Etta with Eric's number. This was it.

"Mary, I have to make an important phone call. I'll tell you everything that happened tonight and dive into all your theories, but Wyatt really messed up something for me, and I have to fix it."

Mary got up. "Okay, I can take a hint. But we're figuring this out, *before* we go to Dad and Lizzie's on Monday."

Anne held up her pinkie. "Absolutely. Pinkie swear."

Mary hooked her pinkie with Anne's and then left, clutching her yearbook and muttering to herself.

Anne immediately pressed on Eric's number and called him. No answer, not that she expected him to answer a late-night call from an unknown number. Her cell number had changed, as had his. Next, she sent him a text.

Can we talk? This is Anne. She added her phone number so he'd know it had been her calling right before that.

But there was no reply to her text and no call back. Anne fell asleep with her phone in her hand, still waiting.

***

After a restless night, Eric finally fell into a deep sleep in the early morning, only waking to the jarring sound of his phone ringing. He should have turned it to silent when he first decided to ignore Anne's text. It was a decision that had him tossing and turning for hours. He felt like a jerk, but it was a move born of self-preservation. He didn't want to hear her explain her relationship with Wyatt. It was none of his business. If that was the kind of guy she was looking for, then whatever.

He dove for his phone on the end of his nightstand before it went to voicemail and swiped to answer. "Hello?"

"Oh, you sound groggy. Never mind."

"Tuttle? I'm fine. What is it?" Eric sat up, feeling more awake as his mind went into work mode. He hadn't had much interaction with Captain Tuttle, as their schedules rarely crossed. Tuttle was usually doing his mandated rest hours while Eric was flying and vice versa.

"I woke up with pink eye of all things. I have the antibiotic drops, and I've already put in my first dose, so I should be good to go for tomorrow when it's been twenty-four hours. Could you take my flights today? You'd have to be in by eight. One flight to Dallas, then over to Austin to pick up three passengers, back here, a flight to Vegas, and back home after the client checks out a property in Henderson. You'll probably wait in Vegas for several hours, but the crew lounge is nice. They have a gym. Or you could sleep."

"Yes, of course." Work sounded perfect right now. When Eric flew, he could shut his mind to all other distractions, focusing solely on the task at hand. Not only that, he wouldn't have to feel guilty about ignoring his phone.

"Great. I'll plan on taking your shift tomorrow, but I'll check in with you tonight. Flight plans are coming over now."

"I'm on it." Eric hung up and headed straight for the shower.

He scrubbed his hair and shaved on autopilot as thoughts of last night bombarded him. All that effort to come to a swanky party as an outsider, to come over and face her family, to befriend her sister. And all the while she was dating Wyatt. He felt like such an idiot.

Eric got dressed, shined his shoes, and grabbed the travel bag he always kept packed and ready by the front door before heading out. On the way to the elevator, he stared at his phone, debating. He needed Anne to know he got her message, but in a way that wouldn't encourage her to keep trying to contact him.

No need to explain. Take care.

After he sent it, he squeezed his phone. That answer was worse than no answer at all. It was like goading her into explaining. He put his phone on airplane mode and stuck it in his inside jacket pocket. There. That way he wouldn't even know if she called again.

It was just until he got back tonight. He could always claim he didn't get something while he was flying. That actually happened a lot. Why he felt he had to justify the decision, he didn't know. He just had this terrible pit in his stomach he wished would go away, and it felt a lot like guilt and regret.

The elevator opened, revealing a woman dressed in scrubs. She eyed him up and down in his pilot uniform as he got in and pressed her lips together, clearly trying to hold back her blatant interest. Another long glance focused on his left hand. No ring. No tan line where a ring used to be. He knew the drill.

"Parking level?" she asked.

"Yep." *Let that be it.* But of course, that was never it. The pilot uniform was a chick magnet. In the months after Anne returned the engagement ring, he had avoided wearing his uniform out in public whenever possible. His coworkers, he didn't have to worry about. Despite the rampant dating between captains and flight crew, he had successfully given off the don't-bother-me vibe, which prevented anyone from getting close to him. The few times he'd attempted a relationship had been disasters. Lucy included.

"Have you lived here long?" She ran her fingers through her hair as she stared straight ahead at the buttons slowly lighting up one by one on the panel.

"Not long."

"I've lived here for three years. I love it here."

Nurses were supposed to be level-headed. She would read his body language and let him be, except she had somehow moved closer to him. One more floor until the parking garage.

She plucked the cap out of his hand and put it on her head, turning to show him how cute it looked on her. "I'm Reesa. Do you want to go out for drinks tonight?"

"No." He reached out for his cap, and she took it off and handed it back. Her face and neck were blotching red, and he felt sorry for embarrassing her. "I'm engaged," he blurted out.

"Congratulations," she squeaked.

The elevator doors swung open, and they both practically ran in opposite directions toward their cars. He got in his sedan and shut the door, a nervous laugh bubbling out of him. Engaged? He'd only said it because he couldn't bear making the poor woman feel completely rejected. But to be honest, he'd always felt like he was still engaged, still tethered to Anne by ties he couldn't break. That deep down he didn't want to break.

Work mode. It was the only thing that had ever helped. He started his car and drove to work.

CHAPTER 13 ♥ I WISH I DIDN'T LOVE HER

Anne stared at her bedroom ceiling and pressed her palms together, her fingers cold against her lips. ***Take care.*** What did Eric mean by that? It was a goodbye, wasn't it? I can't see you anymore so take care of yourself. Was that what he wanted? Not even friendship? She had never been assertive, pushing on the walls people put up to check for weaknesses, attempting another way in. The one week she worked in sales had been nothing less than a stress nightmare. But this wasn't sales, and she couldn't leave it alone. It was too important. She had attempted a call on Sunday morning and Sunday afternoon and one more text.
I'm not dating Wyatt.
No response came, not that she had expected one. And now, this morning she had broken down and called Benneck. He wouldn't even answer until she promised through text not to bring up Lucy. And after confessing everything that happened at the party, Benneck promised to take care of it.

That promise scared her more than anything. Putting Benneck in charge of a reconciliation Eric didn't even want wasn't fair to any of them. Or likely to work. The wait and the worry alone were going to kill her.

She forced herself to get up and do something else, but the embarrassment of it all washed over her again anyway—to have repeatedly reached out, only to get nothing in return. Eric didn't care if she was dating Wyatt or not. She closed her eyes, fighting back tears that pricked the corners of her eyes. From the moment she saw him come around to the side of the cabin to confront her and bring her syrup, the consequences had been unescapable. She knew she would fall for him all over again and get her heart broken. Maybe that was only fair. She'd broken his first.

Mondays were usually busy. She would work a long day at the museum with school groups before coming home and playing with the boys in the backyard, often helping them ruin their appetites for dinner with the snacks they inevitably stole from the kitchen pantry. But today all that would have to be skipped for yet another snobby party Anne couldn't get out of: Lizzie's luncheon to not celebrate her birthday. Lizzie had started up this fun tradition the day she turned thirty, and now every year they were obligated to remember her birthday, but not mention it.

Even if Anne could tell Lizzie and Dad she wasn't coming to brunch, she had already promised Mary she'd go. Mary was still obsessed with her Penelope/Wyatt theories. So far, Anne had been successful in keeping the details of the dinner party about Penelope and Wyatt and leaving Eric out of it, but every time Mary realized she was hearing something new, she wanted to go over it all again, including every conversation Anne had ever had with Wyatt. It was getting harder to keep track of what Anne had told her and what she'd held back.

Anne got ready for the day and walked to the main house, preparing for yet another celebrity gossip update from Mary. But it turned out she didn't have to worry because Mary was busy wrestling Charlie into a kid size suit and tie when Anne walked back to find them. A frustrated Carl chased Colter out the bedroom door and around the great room, shouting threats that had no chance in the universe of being carried out.

"Annie!" Colter, who was in his underwear, jumped off the coffee table and ran for her. "I hate shirts with the tight buttons. They make me gag. We're not going to church or nothing. Why can't I wear regular clothes like you?"

Anne looked down at her jeans and half boots. "You're not wearing clothes at all. Do you plan to go see Grandpa and Aunt Lizzie in your chonies?"

His face lit up. "Can I?"

"No. You can't go in your underwear." Anne looked to Carl to see how much wiggle room she had to work with. Based on Carl's exasperated look, it was a lot. "I'll talk to your mom about clothing options, but you have to say you're sorry to your dad and stop running around like a monkey."

Colter heaved a sigh. "Sorry, Dad." He grabbed Anne's hand and dragged her back down the hall. "Mom! Annie's here. She's going to help me get dressed."

Mary looked up and growled. "Fine. Whatever. Charlie's dress shirt is missing two buttons, and he won't tell me where they are. He probably ate them." She stalked off, leaving Anne with the two boys.

Charlie collapsed back on the bed. His white shirt puffed out where the buttons were missing and he stuck his finger through the opening and poked himself in the belly. "I didn't eat the buttons, I just nibbled on the string part after I pulled the buttons off."

Anne sighed. "Of course you did. Okay, here are the rules. You can't wear anything with words or pictures on it. And you can't wear shorts, and your pants can't have holes. Ready? I'm putting five minutes on my phone. I bet you can't be dressed with shoes on in five minutes. If you're not ready, I'll spin you around until you fall over and call you a rotten egg and tickle you. And ... go!" She sat back against the wall while the boys scrambled to get dressed. Charlie's suit went flying across the room in his excitement to get to wear something else.

Anne looked down at her phone, re-reading Eric's message for the hundredth time and telling herself not to analyze it. She'd been so naïve back when they first broke up, thinking with time they'd both move on and be better apart. He had been her first love, and her first breakup. If only she had known that being the first didn't make it any less real or rare. She would give anything to go back in time and change her decision.

There was a new text message from Wyatt, which she ignored. It actually made her feel worse, thinking maybe Eric considered her text messages and calls as annoying and unwanted as Wyatt's were now that she saw him in a new light.

The timer on her phone went off and she looked up to see both boys standing in front of her, showing off the outfits they'd picked out. In Colter's attempt to follow the rules, he had turned his favorite dinosaur t-shirt inside out to hide the image on the front. Anne looked in his drawer and made him swap it with a nice polo.

Thankfully, Mary and Carl were too tired to do anything but approve, and they all piled into the family SUV. Mary was a stickler about time, just like Dad. They were early, but Mary had to make a stop and pick up Lizzie's gift from a specialty shop before they headed to the condo where Dad and Lizzie were staying. Wyatt's condo. The thought of it now made Anne shudder. At least Wyatt wouldn't be there. He had a conference call he couldn't get out of.

Mary flipped around in her seat and stared at Anne when they were halfway to the shop. "Anne. We didn't finalize a plan. Do we say something to Lizzie?"

"About her birthday?" Carl asked.

Mary waved him away like a gnat. "No, no. This is official sister business. Stay out of it."

Anne shrugged. "We'll just watch Penny and see."

"Who?" Carl asked.

"Shh. No one. I told you not to talk." She turned up the radio and then got out her cell phone and gave Anne a pointed look. Seconds later, Anne got a text message alert. She quickly silenced her phone.

I was thinking about how W made P his door greeter. That's actually important right? It's his house, and he wouldn't want party crashers.

That was a good point. Yes, you had to know the code to get into Wyatt's property, but that didn't mean a sneaky photographer or fan couldn't possibly follow someone inside and try and get in the front door. Who would know guest from stranger better than Penelope, his secret girlfriend? Mary was better at this detective stuff than Anne realized. Except nothing Anne or Mary had found yet proved any of their theories correct, and Anne was feeling more and more detached from caring about it. Anne wished it was true, though. Then maybe her dad and Lizzie would see reason when it came to Penelope. Or knowing them, maybe not.

I don't think Dad or Lizzie will believe us.

Mary frowned at her phone.

We'll have to get proof.

Great. Now Anne would be playing Watson to Mary's Sherlock.

***

Having a rare Monday off, Eric decided to celebrate by sleeping in. Well, that was the version he was going with anyway. It had been just as difficult to fall asleep last night despite a long day of flying, and he was federally mandated to get a good night's rest. This couldn't continue or he wouldn't be able to fly. He squinted at the clock on his nightstand and decided another hour would do it. The sun blocking curtains practically begged him to do it.

Ten minutes later, he was startled awake by the buzzer letting him know he had a visitor downstairs. Sleep would remain an unattainable dream.

He staggered out of bed and over to the box on the wall by the door. "Hello?"

"Since when do you sleep in?"

Apparently, Benneck had finally decided to grace him with his presence.

"I'm not working today. Come up, I'll put pants on."

"I'm flattered."

Eric unlocked his door and went back to his room to throw

on a pair of pajama pants and brush his teeth. Benneck walked in a few minutes later in his uniform, glancing around the apartment and wrinkling his nose. He picked up Eric's water glass from the coffee table and deposited it in the kitchen sink. Eric wasn't a slob, but compared to Benneck he was. It was probably the only thing Benneck and Lucy had in common. Brain injury or not, her apartment always looked perfect.

Eric's little burst of energy upon waking had been used up, and he collapsed on the couch and rubbed his eyes.

"Why didn't you return Anne's calls?" Benneck asked, sitting on the other end.

Eric should have known this was coming. His head felt like it was stuffed with insulation and thoughts of Anne didn't help. "It's complicated."

"It's not complicated. Trust me, I know what complicated is. Lucy is going to be the death of me." Benneck groaned. "Man, I wish I didn't love her."

That had Eric feeling a little more awake. "You love her?"

Benneck looked at the floor, as if the confession cost him dearly. "I do."

"And why does that make you miserable?"

"Do you love Anne?" Benneck asked.

"Don't try to trap me into making a point for you." Eric picked up the remote from the coffee table and turned on the TV. Sports commentary from last night's basketball game came on. Perfect.

"Too late. You do. You love Anne. And you're just as miserable as I am. Point made."

"She's dating Wyatt Ellis. It's a little different."

Benneck stared him down. "No, she's not. He made a pass at her and she removed his hand. The fact that I have to be the messenger for something that could have been easily cleared up by you taking five more seconds before running away tells me you've still got some trust issues. Call her before she gives up on your sorry carcass."

"How do you know all this? Never mind, don't answer that. Let me guess. You and Anne had a sleepover and braided each other's hair last night, talking until morning. Has she helped you figure out what to do about Lucy?"

Benneck punched him in the arm. As usual, it hurt like heck, and Eric totally deserved it. He turned off the TV, stood up, and went to the kitchen to make coffee, rubbing his sore arm. It was hard to get away with wallowing around someone whose heartbreak trumped yours. That was it. Eric needed happier friends. Then he could get away with being the grumpy one.

"Have you had breakfast?" Eric called out.

"Pass! I've seen your fridge. I'm not sure you'd survive if you didn't eat out."

"For a morning person, you're awfully mean." Eric opened his fridge and got out the milk. It was true. Not much else was in there. He wasn't really into big breakfasts. One bowl of cereal and he was out the door every morning.

He poured himself a bowl of corn flakes and enjoyed the quiet until Benneck's next attack. And there would be another attack.

Sure enough, Benneck came to stand in the doorway of the kitchen, looking on with disapproval while Eric rinsed his bowl.

"What exactly did Anne say to you?" Eric asked.

"She said you didn't want to talk to her, and she explained what happened at the party."

"Explained how? What did she say happened?"

"For someone who doesn't return phone calls, you sure are interested in finding out what she had to say."

Eric gave him a dirty look. "Never mind. You're enjoying this too much."

"Okay, okay. I'm sorry. All she said was that you had the wrong idea about them. She said Wyatt stuck his hand on her thigh to be a jerk right when you were saying goodbye to her, and to please tell you she's not dating him."

"That's it?"

Benneck threw up his hands. "What else do you want to know?"

"Why does she want me to know she's not dating him?"

Benneck grinned. "Isn't that the million-dollar question?

You'll have to figure that out yourself. I have to be at the airport soon. I was only stopping by because I promised to check on you." Benneck made a smug departure, swinging Eric's door shut firmly behind him.

Eric turned the lock and kicked the door. He didn't want to be wrong about Anne, because it would mean looking down a long line of stupid, panicky decisions he'd made since leaving the party. But reality didn't care about protecting his feelings, did it? Hope trickled back in as he thought about everything Benneck had said. Terrifying, all-consuming hope. For Eric, hope had always led to hurt in the end. But wasn't he hurting already?

Looking around his apartment with Benneck's disapproving gaze, he grabbed up his broom and dustpan and started picking up the place. He needed somewhere to unleash his nervous energy while his thoughts whirled. Once the front room was picked up, he moved to his bedroom and made his bed. He grabbed his shirt off the floor, the one he'd worn to Wyatt's stupid party, and a slip of folded up paper fell out of the pocket. Lizzie's brunch invitation. The one he thought he'd be working through.

He didn't believe in signs, but if he had, this would be one. Anne wasn't dating Wyatt. He wasn't dating Lucy. They'd been stupid long enough. If he hurried, he would only be a few minutes late. Fashionably late. Wasn't that what celebrities were all about? He dropped the paper on his dresser and went to shower, shave, and get dressed.

CHAPTER 14 ♥ STUPID JEALOUS

"Happy birthday, Aunt Lizzie!" Colter, heedless of, or maybe in purposeful disregard of his mom's warnings, ran in shouting it repeatedly in front of all of Lizzie's friends. They all turned to stare before looking away as if he wasn't there. He might as well have announced he was leprous and planned to touch everyone. Even Beauregard abandoned his perch on the arm of Lizzie's chair and streaked down the hall to one of the bedrooms.

"Colter, get over here this instant." Mary pulled him back by the collar of his polo shirt and knelt down to give him a quiet reprimand eye to eye. She was good at those.

Charlie had stood silently by Anne's side during all of this, and she followed his gaze, quickly realizing why. He stared at the buffet line set up on the far side of the room and then up at Anne. "I'm hungry."

"Come say hello to your grandpa first."

He sighed and allowed Anne to lead him over to where Dad was chatting with several of Lizzie's friends, including Penelope, who was sitting in an arm chair, back straight, nose slightly lifted, giving off the air of holding court.

It all felt exhausting. The worry and pretense of it all. Anne loved her family, but sometimes being with them made her feel more alone than actually, well, being alone.

"Dad, Charlie came to say hello."

"Charlie, my boy." Dad gave him a welcoming smile and a fist bump before turning back to his friends' conversations.

Anne led Charlie away. The kid had his sights set on the food and was happy to be dismissed so easily. Anne helped him get a plate and filled it with pastries and fruit, and he sat on the fireplace hearth and stuffed his face.

The doorbell rang, and Anne heard the murmur of new voices as they were invited in and joined the party. Lizzie passed by, squeezing Anne's shoulder on her way over to check the buffet food. "Thanks for keeping an eye on this little guy."

Anne smiled. Lizzie could be so fun and friendly when she wanted to. Unfortunately, her moods were hard to predict. Charlie's plate began to tilt, and Anne righted it while he finished off his orange juice in a series of long gulps.

"Done," he announced, handing his plate and glass to Anne and then taking off to who knew where. It was no surprise this extra condo of Wyatt's was spacious enough that the word condo didn't really do it justice. She took Charlie's plate to the kitchen, happy to have something to do that would keep her from having to either join a conversation or join Mary in sleuthing. Mary was standing a few feet behind Penelope, eavesdropping.

"Will you bring back a tray of chocolate strawberries?" Lizzie whispered as Anne passed her by.

"Of course." Anne realized with some relief that there was no paid attendant seeing to the food. At least in that regard, Lizzie and Dad were scaling back on things they used to splurge on without a thought.

She tossed the plate in the kitchen garbage and moved to the sink to wash her hands. Turning on the water and getting a pump of soap, Anne hummed to herself. Soon she could go home and take the boys on in a game of soccer in the back yard. They were finally getting to an age where their soccer games didn't consist of kids running in the wrong direction or picking dandelions in the goalie box. Colter was getting better with his passes.

"Anne."

She glanced back to see Eric leaning against the cupboards. He came forward and turned off the water she left running, his chest brushing up against her back. What had she been doing a second ago? Oh, washing her hands. Right. He handed her a towel, and she managed to dry her hands, even though she couldn't stop staring up at him.

"What are you doing here?"

He ducked his head. "Hopefully righting a wrong."

What did that mean? Had he snuck into this party just to talk to her? Anne heard Lizzie calling her name, asking about the strawberries, and on instinct, she pushed Eric into the open pantry and shut the door right before Lizzie walked in.

"I'm bringing them right now." Anne grabbed up the tray of strawberries, following Lizzie out. She put the strawberries down before picking up the mostly empty tray it was replacing. "I'll take this back to the kitchen," she announced to pretty much no one. Lizzie had already put down the pitcher of orange juice she'd retrieved from the kitchen and was back to mingling.

Anne raced back to the kitchen, set the tray on the counter, and pulled open the pantry door where Eric was still standing, looking at her with one eyebrow raised.

"Is there a reason you needed me to hide?" he asked.

Anne shook her head, not knowing how to answer that. Yes, she wanted to hide him from her family, but not because she was ashamed. She wanted time. After not hearing from him since the party, she thought she might never see him again.

Eric smiled. "Okay, well, two can play at this game." He grabbed her hand and pulled her into the pantry with him, shutting the door behind her. Anne reached for the light switch, but thought better of it, afraid someone would walk in the kitchen and see their feet under the door.

In the dark, all her other senses came alive. The pantry smelled faintly like garlic and sugar, but Anne honed in on the scent of Eric, the cologne he was wearing, and the warmth coming off his body. It was tying her throat in knots, not that she had thought of what to say even if she could speak. She swayed a little, and his hands came to rest on her waist, steadying her.

"I was invited, you know," he whispered into her ear.

"Invited where?" she managed to squeak out. "Into this pantry?"

He laughed. "To this party. Although, yes. You invited me into this pantry. Why were you trying to hide me?"

"You said you came to talk to me."

"So, you thought I was a party crasher? I'm hurt, Anne."

He was teasing, but at those words she looked up at his face. In the dark, she could only see the outline of it, his strong jaw, the straight line of his nose. "I'm sorry about Wyatt's party. He's such a toad. And my father and sister, they just don't think before they speak. They've never considered why that would be a good idea."

"It's okay. I'm sorry I didn't call you back."

"Why didn't you?"

He was silent for almost a minute. "Because I was stupid jealous and I jumped to conclusions. Because I felt like a fool for coming to that party at all. For trying again. I feel like a fool now, but there are worse things in life than being foolish."

Anne swallowed hard. "I agree. Sometimes I do foolish things."

She reached up on her tiptoes and wrapped her arms around his neck. His mouth came down on hers, tender at first, but quickly growing in intensity until she thought she might burst with the sensation of it. Kissing Eric was like a favorite memory coming back to life. He pressed her against the pantry door, her head making a little clunking sound when it hit.

She silently laughed and kissed him again, knowing a thousand kisses would never make up for all the time they'd lost.

He pulled away first, running his hands down her arms. "I'm so scared. Sometimes I miss you so much."

"Me too. What are we doing, Eric?"

"I don't know." His forehead pressed against hers.

She tilted her head up to kiss him again, but the pantry door abruptly opened, and she tumbled out, saving her backside only by catching the floor with her hands. Eric caught himself just in time not to join her.

"What is going on?" Dad's voice boomed out. "Anne? Get up." He not-so-delicately pulled her up from the floor and turned to glare at Eric.

"Why are you here? Nobody invited you. Anne, did you sneak him into your sister's bir— er bruncheon? He scowled at his own slip of the tongue and pointed toward the kitchen door. "Out, young man. Get out of my house."

It was a twisted repeat of eight years ago, but Anne was not twenty anymore and she feared losing Eric a lot more than she feared being wrong about love.

"Dad. Stop. This isn't even your house, and he was invited here. Eric. Stay."

Several people ducked their heads in the kitchen to have a peek before going back to the urgent whispering she could hear on the other side of the wall. It didn't matter. Embarrassment was only a small buzzy thing way off in the corner of her mind, easily ignored.

She turned to Eric. "I thought if enough time passed I'd stop missing you, but I never did. Never." She had to get the words out before she lost her chance. Dad's arm hadn't dropped from where it was pointing toward the door. He wouldn't be backing down.

Eric reached out and touched her cheek. "I'm gonna go, Anne. It's okay. I promise. Make it a good party for your sister." With his hands in his pockets, he walked out, thanked Lizzie for inviting him, and left.

CHAPTER 15 ♥ DEAR, ANNE

Eric ran out of the building hopped up on pure adrenaline and blinding happiness. It was quite the power kick. And yet, knowing that leaving Anne there was the best way to de-escalate the situation didn't make it any easier. She would be facing her family alone, after having fallen out of a pantry while secretly making out with her ex. Anne was usually the one defusing drama, not causing it.

He jumped in his car, drummed his hands across his steering wheel, at moments so full of joy he felt like it might burst out of him, and at others filled with worry. However dysfunctional, Anne's family was important to her. He saw the way those nephews of hers looked to her for guidance, in a sort of hero worship that was so important to little boys at their age.

Eric did not want to be the cause of an irrevocable rift, a gulf leaving Anne on one side with her family on the other, choosing love over family. Sometimes relationships were so toxic a person had no choice, but Anne would have to be the judge of that, not him.

That's when the truth of eight years ago hit him like a train. He had always looked at Anne choosing to side with her family over him as a total betrayal, but he never should have put her in an all-or-nothing position in the first place. He should have done a better job of supporting her, waiting for her to be ready instead of worrying about the looming deadline of when they'd go long-distance if she didn't run off and marry him.

He drove home and paced around his apartment for several minutes before getting out a sheet of paper and sitting down to write Anne a letter. She was too good for him, for anyone, really, and the pain of realizing what a complete idiot he had been was only outweighed by deep gratitude for getting a second chance with her.

If he tried to tell it all to her in person, she would stop him and say all was forgiven before he could get the words out. There would also probably be some intense kissing getting in the way as well. That thought-bunny almost derailed him completely. But Anne deserved to know how wonderful she was. She didn't hear it often enough.

He wrote a few sentences before crumpling up the paper and tossing it off his desk. He had thought it was a stupid thing people only did in movies, crumpling up a paper, but it was a strangely satisfying way of guaranteeing he would have to try again.

He began on a new sheet, and this time the words flowed.

Dear Anne,

I panicked when I saw you at the Musgrove's cabin. I spent eight years trying to forget you, and seeing you again was the truth coming to let me know how bad a job of it I did. Men are stupid when it comes to their egos, and when you gave me back my ring, I didn't stick around long enough to find out why you were rejecting me. I made my own conclusions, ones that put you in a bad light. The pain was too much to do otherwise, and when the pain was replaced by regret I turned it into blame because it was easier to live with.

I would have done it a second time if you hadn't reached out through our horrible mutual friend. Though I will hate

Benneck's gloating until my dying day, I'm glad he never stopped trying to get me to see what was right in front of me. You have always been right in front of me, constantly in my thoughts until fate threw us together again. That sounds romantic until I think about how I might have made that choice myself. Fate is for those unwilling to act. I should have come back. I should have called. I should have crawled to you on my knees and begged you to let us start over. But instead, I stubbornly tried to make a life without you. It was a half-life, in every sense of the word.

You are a rare beauty, inside and out. I have never known anyone as wonderful, as kind, or as unique as you are, sweet Anne. You make everything better and everyone better for having spent time with you.

I have a lot to learn, but one thing I know is I love you with my whole soul. If you tell me I'm too late, I'll still love you and trust you know what's best this time. But if you want me here, I'm yours forever.

Always,
Eric

With the letter sealed and in hand, he locked the apartment door behind him and ran to the elevator. He would leave it for Anne at her door, so when she returned home after a, no-doubt, utterly uncomfortable family meeting, she'd have his words until they could see each other again.

The elevator dinged and opened, revealing the same forward woman in the scrubs, only this time there were several other people, too. Not in his uniform, it took her a few seconds before she recognized him. If embarrassment had a face, it was hers. She looked like she wanted to become one with the wall the second their eyes met.

"How are you today?" He asked.

"Fine." She blinked several times and fidgeted with the purse in her hands. "And you?"

"It's a great day, actually. It might go down as the best one of all time. At least until tomorrow."

Several people smiled at him in that indulgent way one might humor a mime on the streets of San Francisco. He probably sounded like something out of a musical, but he didn't care.

"Reesa, isn't it?"

She glanced at the woman standing next to her and then down at her feet. "Um, yeah."

"Do you two know each other?" the woman asked. "I'm Reesa's roommate. I don't think we've met."

Eric didn't say anything, enjoying the awkwardness a little too much. With such a light heart, pretty much everything seemed funny to him.

"I met him on the elevator yesterday," Reesa finally admitted.

Her friend gasped. "Wait, is this the … pilot?" She began cackling, looking from Eric's grinning face to Reesa's mortified one.

Eric turned and saluted before getting off. "Bye, ladies." He jogged to his car and got in. He had a letter to deliver.

***

Anne wasn't sure when she'd seen Mary look more alive and in her element. For the first time in Mary's life, she was the rational sister in a situation, the one asking everyone else to calm down.

All the other guests had been sent home, and the little boys were off watching TV in one of the bedrooms. Carl, a pacifist through and through, had decided to join them.

The powder keg that had been building ever since Eric left was about to go off. Anne could feel it. If there was a family rule the Elliots lived by, it was don't make a scene in public. Scratch that, only make a scene in public if you mean to do it, and only if it will elevate the family's standing. As Anne hadn't meant to share her happy moment with the entire non-birthday party, she was therefore breaking the rule several times over.

Mary patted Lizzie's hand. "It was still a nice party," she murmured.

"No thanks to you," Dad said, rounding on Mary suddenly. "Why didn't you get a babysitter for the boys? No one else brought children."

Mary glared up at him. "You said it was a family party. They're family. I didn't know half the people here."

"Yes, but *I* did. And they're not the sort of people who like to see children running under foot."

"Dad," Lizzie said softly. "Don't take this out on Mary. She's only trying to help, and at least she made an effort to meet people. Anne was the one who was supposed to be watching the boys." Her expression chilled when it moved to Anne.

Dad rounded on her as well. "I can't believe you would ruin your sister's party this way. You left the boys alone with all the guests, and they knocked over Penelope's mimosa. Penelope had to scrub an arm chair before a stain could set in, *during* the party!" He turned a sympathetic gaze to Penelope, who smiled back up at him.

Mary glanced at Anne and nodded, as if to say, *we'll get to that*. Dad was just winding up, and wouldn't listen to anything until he had his say.

"And as for Eric Wentworth, what kind of man lures a woman into a kitchen pantry for a clandestine meeting? All it did was draw attention to my own daughters moving in and out of the kitchen, catering their own party, as if we couldn't afford staff to replenish the buffet station for us."

Lizzie nodded. "So humiliating."

Anne had had enough. "Eric Wentworth is the kind of man who cares about me, despite the fact that my family treats him like dirt. You ran him off years ago because he didn't fit in. But I don't want him to fit in. He's perfect the way he is. He's perfect for me. And I'm sorry the party didn't turn out the way you hoped, but I'm not the reason. Dad, you're the one who came in and pulled me out of the pantry and made a scene. You ruined the party."

Dad's mouth gaped open and closed like a fish. "I didn't know you were in the pantry. How was I supposed to know that? I heard a noise."

"But you reacted very badly. And I forgive you." Anne was sweating, and yet so cold she couldn't help shaking. She blinked and centered herself. "I forgive you for everything, but I'm not bringing Eric back here unless you can be nice."

"Be nice?" Dad echoed with a snort, looking around to see who else thought Anne was being ridiculous.

Anne's sisters both stared at her in wonder. Penelope looked bored.

There was a long silence before Dad sniffed. "Eric can come if he's invited. I'll have to discuss it with Lizzie and Penelope. I don't think we'll be hosting another party any time soon. I need to test the waters and see what sort of a splash we made today. People easily move onto other gossip when something better comes along. We just need someone to go into rehab or something."

He continued, but Anne tuned much of it out, instead listening to what she thought might be footsteps approaching the front door. She stood, meaning to go check, just as keys turned in the lock.

Wyatt came in, whistling a happy tune to himself. "Sorry I missed it. How was the party?"

No one answered.

"That good, eh. What did I miss?"

Dad scowled. "I found Anne in the pantry with Eric Wentworth where they were…"

"Kissing," Anne filled in for him. She wasn't about to wait for his description of it. "We were kissing."

Wyatt's eyebrows raised. "Well, that sounds like my kind of party. Guess I know why Anne's been ignoring my texts now." He winked at her, before his eyes turned to Penelope for the briefest of seconds.

Mary cleared her throat. "I've been meaning to ask. Wyatt, you graduated from high school with Lizzie and Penelope, didn't you? Are there any pictures of the three of you together? Were you all friends then?"

Lizzie gave a nervous laugh. "Sometimes we were besties, and sometimes we were stabbing each other in the back. That's high school."

What kind of answer was that? Anne glanced at Mary, who looked just as confused.

Mary raised her eyebrows. "Backstabbing? Do tell. I think we could all use a good story right about now. Poor Anne's not used to being the center of attention. We might give her a panic attack if we're not careful."

Everyone had a good laugh at Anne's expense. No one except Anne saw it for what it was, a thinly-veiled dig for information. Wow, Mary was good at this.

Wyatt scratched the back of his head. "I don't know what Lizzie's talking about. I never backstabbed anyone."

Lizzie shrugged. "Except for that time you told me you had to break our study date at the library, but when I went to search the stacks for my assigned book, I found you doing a little research in the Visual Arts section with Penelope."

Mary gripped the arm of the chair she was sitting in, looking like she was about to jump out of it. This was it. All her research was about to pay off.

Wyatt scoffed. "I hooked up with a lot of girls back there. Like you said, it was high school."

That answer seemed to satisfy Lizzie, but Penelope looked livid. "Is that so?"

Wyatt turned to study an impressionist painting on the wall. "A guy shouldn't kiss and tell."

"And now you're all such good friends," Mary said brightly, looking around at all of them. "That's nice that you can set the past aside, especially with Dad dating Penelope. I would never be able to do that."

"Didn't Carl go out with Anne before you?" Lizzie asked, looking way too innocent.

"It was one date!" Carl hollered from the other room. "I never kissed her. I never even thought about kissing her. We went out for pizza."

Anne glanced at Mary, worried she would take Lizzie's hook like a good fish, but Mary looked calm. She'd save that grudge for another day, no doubt. "I believe you, dear," she hollered back. "Nobody would kiss you after you eat pepperoni pizza. Not even me."

"Penelope and I aren't dating," Dad said quietly. "It's just a game we play to keep up appearances. A real relationship is too much work when I'm trying to restart my career. She makes beautiful arm candy, though, doesn't she?" He smiled at her, and Penelope smiled back.

Mary seemed to deflate like a balloon. All that worry for nothing. Well, not for nothing. There was no need to fear Dad would marry her, but Penelope was still working the situation for all she could, with Dad and Lizzie none the wiser.

"Are you ready to go?" Anne asked Mary. Somewhere, Eric was waiting for her, and these petty dramas would still be here the next time Anne visited her family. There was no need to wallow in it today.

Mary nodded, hollering, "Boys, we're leaving."

Anne gave Dad and Lizzie each a hug and left with a little boy holding tightly to each of her hands.

CHAPTER 16 ♥ A GET-TO-KNOW-YOU BUCKET LIST

Eric played with his water glass, occasionally scanning the people walking past the café window. Normally, people-watching would interest him, but now all he saw was people who weren't Anne. He wasn't impatient, but that didn't mean he wasn't eager. After eight years without her, he was ready to make things right.

His phone buzzed with a text, and he looked down to check it. *No more waiting.*

He felt a tap on his shoulder. "If anyone has been living a half-life, it's me."

Eric whirled around and stood to catch Anne up in a hug. She was really and truly here, flesh and blood. She'd come. He relaxed his hold, afraid he was crushing her, but she held on tighter and her shoulders began to shake.

"Don't cry now, my sweet Anne. I'll think it's my fault."

"It is your fault," she choked out with a laugh. "But I'm happy crying this time."

He leaned back enough to wipe her tears away, and if they hadn't been standing in the middle of a crowded café, he would have kissed away every single tear that followed.

Asking her to meet him at the café next door to his

apartment building had been a last-minute request scribbled on the back of the envelope he left her at her door. He had been sitting here for over an hour, and he would've waited until the place closed if that was how long it took for her to work out things with her family.

He pulled out her chair and sat across from her at the table he'd claimed. He'd had to defend her seat from chair snatchers several times in the past hour, although putting Anne on his lap until they could steal one back wouldn't have been a terrible option.

"Are you hungry?" he asked.

Anne shook her head. "Lizzie might have been angry with us when we left, but there was no way she was keeping all the leftover pastries. She ran them down to Carl and Mary right before we drove away. She sent all the chocolate strawberries too. Mary and I ate quite a few after we got back while we talked everything over." Anne laughed. "I think the only person who truly enjoyed today was Mary. She lives for gossip."

"Well, I'm glad we could provide her some."

"We're only the half of it. Mary and I finally figured out what Wyatt Ellis has been up to this whole time. I could never figure out why he and Dad were friends at all, or why he began texting me constantly after I met him at the storage place."

Eric felt a kick to his gut thinking about how he had refused to come that day. "I should have been there."

Anne shook her fist. "I knew Benneck called you, the little sneak. I told him not to. I guess there's no need to be embarrassed about that now."

"I should be embarrassed. I was neck deep in denial about you, and somehow thought dating one of Mary's sisters-in-law would help."

Anne pulled out her phone and unlocked it, turning to show him. "I have pages and pages of texts back and forth with Wyatt about the most meaningless things. I thought he wanted to be friends." She shook her head as if the idea was preposterous.

"Why are you convinced Wyatt wasn't actually interested in you, Anne?" She had always been modest, but this was too much. "I personally think he lost his head a little when it came to you. Why do you think he sat me at a table away from the two of you at dinner?"

Anne's eyes widened. "I thought you didn't want to sit with my family."

"I'd want to sit with you no matter who you had at the table. That's why I came over after, when the guy next to you left."

He could almost see Anne's brilliant mind unlocking all the pieces she had seen as certain and rearranging them. "Wyatt didn't want you there so he would be free to flirt with me and fling it in Penelope's face. It all makes sense now. I bet he took screen shots of our texts back and forth and sent them to her. How despicable. Oh, wow. I'm sounding like Mary now with her conspiracy theories, aren't I?"

Eric laughed. "Um, no. I love Mary, but you don't sound like her. Anne, when I said you make everyone better, that wasn't a line I was throwing out. You and Mary are complete opposites, and yet you accept each other as you are. You don't tolerate her like everyone else does. You bring out the good in her."

Anne's cheeks took on a beautiful blush, but she was saved from saying anything because a harried waitress approached. "Can I get you anything, miss?"

Anne shook her head.

The waitress, with a look of disgruntled patience, turned to Eric. "Can I top off your water, sir?"

It was Eric's turn to be embarrassed. While waiting for Anne, he'd been too keyed up to eat a thing. "Actually, I think we're good. Here's your tip." He got out a twenty dollar bill and handed it over.

The waitress rolled her eyes and left, though she looked a lot less irritated.

Anne squeezed his hand. "We should probably get out of here."

Together they walked out, and once on the sidewalk, Eric pointed out the apartment building towering over the little café. "That's where I live. I'm on the fifth floor."

Anne tugged on his hand. "Come show me. I want to see

your place." He laughed as she broke into a jog, pulling him along in her excitement.

They had the elevator to themselves, and Anne took a minute to catch her breath before wrapping her arms around his waist and tucking her head into the crook of his neck. It was familiar and new all at the same time. He used to hold her like this while they waited in line at the movies on Friday nights. The thought of having her with him always, to hold, to talk to, to dream with, it all hit him like a tidal wave, and he tipped her head up and pressed his lips to hers.

She met his kiss with a little sigh, standing up on her tiptoes to better reach him. When she smiled, he moved his kisses to the corner of her mouth, and then her jaw, and then the soft underside of her ear.

The elevator dinged, and he reluctantly released her, not wanting to irritate the half a dozen people waiting to get on. There were several knowing smirks thrown their way, but Anne only laughed and followed him out and down the hall to his apartment.

He unlocked his door and watched while Anne wandered around looking at things.

"I feel like I know you," she said, "And yet, I have all this catching up to do. You have a nice couch now." She picked up his uniform cap from off the kitchen table and ran her fingers over the gold emblem before trying it on. It was too big for her and came halfway down her forehead.

"What is it with women and a man in uniform?" He came over and ducked down so he could give her a quick kiss under the cap. "A woman actually pulled it out of my hands the other day and put it on her head before asking me if I wanted to go out for drinks. On that elevator." He pointed towards the door.

Anne laughed. "You seem to get a lot of action on that elevator, young man. What did you tell her?"

"I told her I was engaged." He said it with a laugh, but they both sobered the longer they stared at each other. His heartbeat thundered in his ears. Anne was his everything. "I want to marry you, Anne." He didn't want to tiptoe around it or ever make her wonder where she stood with him.

Anne stared back before turning and walking into his living room. She set the hat on the arm of the couch and sunk into a cushion, tucking her legs in as if she had always belonged there. "You always were a fast mover."

He laughed. "What kind of answer is that?"

She patted the spot next to her on the couch and he willingly complied.

Lacing her fingers with his, she gazed at him intently. Her eyes were pools of blue he had always loved getting lost in, now more than ever. "I love you and I want to marry you. Never doubt that. But I'm not going anywhere. Be here with me. Right here, right now. We don't have to make up for lost time, because that would be dwelling on what we've lost. Tell me about all the places you've traveled. Tell me about how you met Benneck. Tell me where you got this couch because it's so comfortable and beautiful. Mary's searching for a new one. The boys jump on her cushions, and now it has this terrible sag that makes your bum feel completely lopsided when you sit on it."

Eric rested his head back and closed his eyes, focusing on the warmth of Anne's fingers against his. "I don't know where to start. My mom bought the couch as a welcome gift when I moved here. I'll have to ask her where she got it from."

"Where does your mom live these days? Oh, I miss her. She was always so sweet."

He'd forgotten about that. His mom would be so happy to hear about Anne, although to be honest, she'd be happy to hear he had anyone in his life. "It really is like we've always known each other, and yet we're starting over. We need a list." He got up and retrieved scratch paper from his desk. "We need to make a catch-up list."

Anne eyed him with amused suspicion.

"I know, I know you said we don't have to make up for lost time, so think of this as a get-to-know-you bucket list." He wrote down, *Road trip to see Mom.* "She's in Oregon on an extended summer vacation. She has a boyfriend there who has been trying to get her to marry him for five years. But she loves her house and her yard and her knitting group, and he has grown kids who don't like the thought of their dad remarrying. He's rich, and they're afraid he'll change his will." Eric looked up. "You're not going to make me wait another five years, are you?"

Anne shook her head at him. "I'm patient, but I'm not that patient." She stole the paper and added *Tour the Natural History Museum*. "You should see where I work."

"Of course. And you should see mine. I want to fly you somewhere. Where would you want to go?"

Anne blushed. "You'll think it's dumb."

"Why would I think it's dumb?"

She shrugged. "My friend Beth and I—Beth works at the museum with me. We've been talking about someday going to see the Ashfall Fossil Beds. It's a state park in Royal, Nebraska. They have prehistoric camels and rhinos and horses. And hiking trails..." She got a wistful look.

Eric took the paper and pen out of her hand and wrote *Meet Beth. Crash girl trip to go see old fossils.*

Anne laughed. "I promise what I do is not as boring as you think."

"I don't think your job is boring." Even as he said it, he remembered poking fun at her love of dinosaurs when he was a stupid twenty-one-year-old. "Wait here." He hopped up and went to his bookshelf, touching each of the spines until he found the one he was looking for. He handed Anne the two-inch thick book.

"The Encyclopedia of Dinosaurs." She looked up at him. "When did you get this?"

He rubbed the back of his neck. He'd wanted her to ask, and yet it made him feel a little bit vulnerable to admit it out loud. "I'd been studying up on your favorite dinosaurs as a surprise. After we broke up, I chucked it in the garbage when I was moving my things out of my apartment. I was angry and hurting. That one you're holding is a copy I came across about a year ago. It was on top of a stack of bargain books, and I can't even explain why I bought it again. I guess I just felt bad about throwing out the old one, even though you weren't there to see it."

A tear rolled down Anne's cheek, and he reached out, catching it right before it fell off the edge of her jaw. She gazed up at him, her expression changing from sorrow to something almost mischievous the longer they stared at one another. She took his hand and pulled him back down next to her on the couch.

"Is this a list thing?" he asked, smiling as she leaned in, running her fingers up his arm and stopping at a thin white scar just above his elbow.

"Think of this as a get-to-know-you inspection. What's this from?"

"I wish I could say it was something manly, like chopping wood or racing motorcycles. I backed into a weight machine at the gym."

Her eyes widened. "You didn't."

"Don't laugh." It didn't matter, she was already laughing and he couldn't help laughing too. "You're turn. Confess."

"You've already seen me do plenty of embarrassing things, Eric."

"Adorable things."

"We'll agree to disagree on that one."

He traced his finger over her palm, wanting to kiss her, but holding back so he didn't cut off whatever she might be about to say.

She must have been reading his mind because she leaned in and kissed him anyway. There was less urgency this time, but definitely more joy. Anne kissed with her whole heart. He could feel it, the surety of being loved by her. He would never take it for granted again.

They held each other and talked until the soft light filtering through the window changed and dimmed, and logic took hold. Her car would be towed from the café parking lot if they didn't go get it.

But there was always tomorrow. And the next day. And the next. For the first time in a long time, the future looked bright.

EPILOGUE ♥

"This is your captain speaking. I hope you're enjoying your journey in our Gulfstream G150 today. We have clear skies all the way to our destination at Norfolk Regional Airport. The temperature there is a lovely sixty-eight degrees, and we'll be landing in approximately forty-five minutes to begin our fossil hunt bucket list expedition. In a moment, my co-captain with me today, Benneck James, will be taking the controls for me while I come back to the cabin to kiss my beautiful wife."

Anne laughed at the polar reactions from the women sitting across from her. Lucy was practically swooning, while Beth looked both amused and disgusted, all while never taking her eyes from the knitting needles flying between her fingers. She was making an ill-shaped coaster, which the men had already repeatedly made fun of despite Anne's protests that Beth was doing really well for a beginner knitter.

Beth and Benneck often squabbled like brother and sister, and with that came moments of hilarity and moments when it was best to separate them. This trip would be an interesting one, for so many reasons.

"You know, he could just turn around and holler that announcement and we'd hear him." Beth wrinkled her nose. "But I guess it wouldn't sound quite as sexy."

Lucy sighed. "No, no, it wouldn't. You're so lucky, Anne. I wish Benneck and I were already married. Sometimes I think I'd like to do what you did and have a small, simple ceremony, but then I think about my dress, and the eight-piece orchestra, and the limo, and the crystal centerpieces."

"That sounds like a nightmare," Beth quipped. At Lucy's shocked response she quickly added, "A nightmare to plan. It sounds like a nightmare to plan. But I'm sure it's going to be beautiful and amazing, and I'm so happy for you."

Lucy looked somewhat mollified, but she'd never really understood Beth's dry sense of humor to begin with. Lucy craned her neck around Anne to try to see into the cockpit. "Those two. I bet Eric can't come back here because Benneck's talking his ear off. You'd think with all their hours flying together they'd run out of things to say."

Anne looked up from her book. "Benneck doesn't run out of things to say to anybody."

Lucy and Beth both laughed.

"So, Beth," Lucy said, turning to her with a coy look. "How come you didn't bring..." The longer she took to finish her question, the more panicked she looked.

"You can't remember his name," Beth said. "There's your answer right there. Our relationship is too new, and he barely knows you guys. Besides, I'm not afraid to be a fifth wheel." Beth gave Anne a secret smile. They'd discussed this a lot while planning the trip. If anyone was a tag-along, it was Lucy and Benneck, who would probably ditch out on their dinosaur expedition to stay back at the hotel and watch movies.

"What happened with Penelope and Wyatt, Anne?" Lucy asked, clearly relieved to see Beth didn't look offended.

It was the perfect subject change, though not one Anne would have brought up on her own.

"It's a mess, to be honest." That got their attention, though she couldn't fault their interest. It was all anyone who cared about Hollywood gossip was talking about at the moment.

"After the paparazzi got that photo of Wyatt and Penelope kissing in his car, there was no need for all the secrecy anymore, or for my dad or Lizzie to stay with her at his condo. So, they're back in Malibu, trying to avoid the press. And as far as I know, Penelope is still living in Wyatt's condo, loving having it all to herself, no doubt."

Anne's interest in it only went as far as her dad and sister's involvement. She left Lucy and Beth to their endless speculation, letting her mind wander to other things, like ancient watering holes, and prehistoric rhinos, and when her husband would be coming to say hello.

When her ears caught the slight whooshing sound of someone walking up the aisle, she closed the book she hadn't really had a chance to read and jumped up to catch Eric in a hug. Taking his hand, she dragged him over to a plush leather chair out of Lucy and Beth's view and sat on his lap, wrapping her arms around his neck. He smelled so good and his smile of surprise was so inviting that she gave into temptation and kissed him quite thoroughly before remembering where they were.

"Sorry, I know we promised we weren't going to do this to everyone. We've already had a honeymoon. Two if you count the weekend trip to Catalina Island." She ran her hand across the back of his hair, playing with the ends that were beginning to curl where they met his neck. It was almost time for him to get a haircut. "Maybe we shouldn't have planned this group trip so soon after getting married. I'm having a really hard time keeping my hands off of you."

"Anne!" He laughed against her neck. "Shh. What's gotten into you? And are you saying in a few years you'll no longer be tempted by my masculine wiles?"

"Masculine wiles?" She tugged on the lapels of his coat. "I've never heard of those. You'll have to explain them to me."

His face got a little red, but he met her gaze with his best smolder, which would have worked better if he wasn't fighting to keep a straight face. "You know, they're like feminine wiles. Those things you have that cause me to double-time it up the stairs instead of taking the elevator when it's busy, so I can have as much time as possible with you after I get off work."

"Oh, those wiles," Anne whispered. "I understand those.

And when I'm too old to even single-time it up any stairs, I will still love you, and I'll still want you, Eric."

"Hey," Benneck hollered from the cockpit. "Are you done kissing your wife yet? We have a jet to land, lover boy."

"Be right there." Eric gave Anne one last kiss before helping her off his lap. "Ready for an adventure?"

She looked through the oval window at the clear blue sky. "So ready."

Thank you, readers! I so love playing with Jane Austen's amazing characters. Reviews are much appreciated. If you'd like to hear about new releases, you can follow my Amazon author page: www.amazon.com/author/racheljohn

Other titles by Rachel John:

Engaging Mr. Darcy
Emma the Matchmaker
Dashing into Disaster

Worst Neighbor Ever
I Hated You First
Carpool Crush

An Unlikely Alliance
Her Charming Distraction
Protector of Her Heart
Pretending He's Mine

Matchmaker for Hire
Bethany's New Reality
Gorgeous and the Geek

The Stand-in Christmas Date
The Christmas Bachelor Auction
The Christmas Wedding Planners
The Accidental Christmas Match Up

Manufactured by Amazon.ca
Bolton, ON